ERIN BENDER

The Treasure of Amidon

Rory Foresman

Copyright © 2022 Rory Foresman
All rights reserved.
ISBN: 9798412351490

FORWARD

If you're traveling through North or South Dakota, you might be traveling US Hwy 85 south to the Black Hills or north toward Canada. Many travelers use this route to visit the little tourist town of Medora, ND where Teddy Roosevelt was a cowboy and rancher in the 1800s. For whatever reason you travel Highway 85, you will ultimately pass through the little North Dakota town of Amidon.

Boasted as once the smallest county seat in the nation, Amidon now has competition from Brewster, Nebraska, Mentone, Texas, and Gann Valley, South Dakota, based on the 2010 through 2013 census.

What makes this little town so attractive to travelers? It might be the close proximity to the highest point in North Dakota, White Butte; or the Burning Coal Vein to the west as you enter into the Badlands; or perhaps it's enjoying a cold beer at Mo's Bunker Bar - a favorite saloon stop for bikers on their way to the Sturgis motorcycle rally in the Black Hills of South Dakota.

These all are great reasons to frequent the area. However, they're not the subject of conversation when passing through Amidon. What locals and travelers alike recall most is the old police cruiser with a cop mannequin waiting in eternal limbo as a deterrent for speeders who slam on their brakes when the police cruiser is spotted.

What you experience in North Dakota will be remembered and talked about for years to come.

Learn more about Amidon at the end of this adventure.

Thank you to those who spent so much time reading and editing. To my brothers, Chan and Ryan. To my wonderful and helpful wife, Rosanne. And to my good friend, John Morrison.

CHAPTER 1

Erin quickly moved to the outside of the door, her back to the wall. She held a hard-shell case in one hand, a leather bag in the other, and a tripod under her arm; she glanced over at Emeric.

"Are we clear?"

"All clear," Emeric replied.

Erin went through the door opening. Working her way to the center of the room, she glanced around at the interior. Not much different than the other old-world buildings they had scavenged. This particular building had once been a bar, raided many times by Marauders or other lawless men; it showed damage and wear.

The bar was busted up and full of bullet holes; tables and chairs were broken and scattered. Small fragments of the mirror still lined the back of the bar. Erin placed the case on the floor without a word and began setting up the tripod, a routine she's completed dozens of times. Initially, the Light Bender could be rolled on the floor and have a room scanned in seconds. However, what they were looking for would take much longer to find.

The Light Bender, as Erin named it, was a scanning device. A round-shaped orb – a sophisticated piece of technology from the old world. Technology had become so advanced militant countries went to war over it. Each believed their technology was superior, and destroying another country's technology would give them domination over the world. That was over 50 years ago. No one knows who started it or if anyone won. Stories became myths; myths became legends, and all that remained was the remnant of a scorched planet.

Emeric was standing just inside the doorway, keeping watch. At no time could he let his guard down. That would be the moment trouble would come; they had made that mistake more than once in their scavenging career.

"I'm just about set up, Em."

"Still all clear," Emeric whispered loudly.

Once Erin started the scanning process, they would leave the room, allowing the scanner to complete its job; this was the dangerous part of the procedure. Leaving the safety and cover of a building made them an easy target. They hadn't yet taken the time to clear the other buildings in town. She was confident Lucky would be doing that while she worked. The initial scan would only take five minutes.

Five minutes in the open can feel like an eternity when the area hasn't been cleared.

Erin and Emeric quickly slipped out the door; she didn't want their presence to hinder the scan. They moved around the side of the building with their backs to the wall. Both held their guns in a ready position. Erin glanced at the watch on her wrist; they stood in silence.

Erin looked up and down the main street, wondering where Lucky was hiding. No one knew his real name, not even Lucky. He was born in what is referred to as the Wild West. Areas of the Midwest void of populated cities and towns called the Range. Orphaned at a young age, he learned how to survive, hide, and get around virtually undetected. As far back as he could remember, he was called Lucky. Lucky to have survived and lucky at avoiding trouble. He was the best at what he did, and as soon as they had finished scavenging, he would be there waiting for them, horses ready.

Five minutes later, Erin peeked around the corner. Erin gave Emeric the all-clear sign, not seeing anything that looked disturbed, out of the ordinary, or signs of movement. They both moved out from around the front of the building and back through the door. Emeric took the same defensive position at the door as if he had never moved.

The Light Bender turned off; it had finished its initial scan. Erin pulled out a small handheld computer module in its protected padding of the carry case and then turned it on to retrieve the pictures from the scan.

"Probably enough power for one more scan here today; we'll have to head back soon."

Emeric responded with a nod of his head.

Erin had preset the scanner for non-ferrous materials. There has always been a demand for reusable metals such as aluminum, copper, zinc, and lead. All these metals are malleable and easy to make into something new. Gold and Silver had only become popular over the last ten years as knowledge of old-world technology started to advance once again. For the last 50 years, survival remained the priority. Ammo for weapons had always been in high demand. Lead was primarily used to make bullets. Copper and zinc were needed to make the brass casing to keep up with the demand for ammo. Those who could make it or afford to trade for it had a greater chance of survival. With advancements in education and technology, the demand for these metals began to shift.

The Light Bender's scan showed small lead fragments in the walls and around the bar; it wasn't worth the time digging them out. When Erin turned the screen toward the bar, a cluster of shapes showed around the backside. It looked about the size of small boxes of ammo. Only a few scattered traces of colors remained.

The computer didn't show a clear outline, possibly due to the old wood's thickness around the bar; the scanner's sensitivity settings were set at four out of 10. Erin wasn't sure. Erin put down her computer screen and walked around to the back of the bar. Getting down on her knees, she took out her flashlight. She couldn't see anything but old wood. In her experience, however, nothing is as it seems. Feeling around for anything unusual, her finger came across a finger-sized hole.

"Ah-ha," she whispered under her breath.

Putting her finger into the hole, she gave it a downward tug, and a compartment on the underside of the bar pulled open. Erin grabbed the items inside the hidden area, stood up, and laid a revolver and two ammo boxes on top of the bar.

Erin stood there looking at Emeric as if she had made the find of a lifetime. Items they scavenge are referred to as a "Find," The bag she would put them into was called the "Findings Bag." Now, if you'd ask any team member when Erin found something of real value to her, it was like the find of a lifetime.

What she desired, however, were words of affirmation.

Emeric glanced over, looked at the gun and ammo, nodded his head, and said, "can always use more ammo."

Erin didn't reply; she just got that silly offended look on her face, you know, the one that says… that's not the response I wanted!

Erin picked up the gun and ammo and put them into their Findings Bag lying on the floor. "Not enough battery power to do another non-ferrous scan in this room. I'll do a preliminary search of the rest of the rooms on the next floor to determine our next scan."

"You know where to find me." A typical response from Emeric.

Erin quickly walked through each of the rooms, looking for anything unusual. She didn't notice anything out of place, but that didn't mean something wasn't there.

Over the years, the survivors found very creative ways of hiding anything they thought was of value. Scavengers would take down an entire building piece by piece, searching for valuables. Erin's scanner, the Light Bender, gave her the advantage. It made it easier to find these hidden gems. They could come back again to scan these rooms and the rest of this abandoned town another time. Erin had estimated earlier they could have this little town scanned and scavenged in about five days. If this initial scan turned out well, they would move their base camp to Amidon and secure the area.

Erin came back down from the second floor to the room once used as an office. It would be the most logical place to scan at this time and the most likely place to find coins and other Findings. Coins had no value as currency, only traded for their mineral content. The copper, zinc, and nickel could be melted down for repurposing. Paper money had once been called legal tender, and although coins were valuable, paper money was not. The old-timers would say that paper money never was worth anything. Scavengers just called it tinder; good for starting a fire or wiping paper.

Just then, a whistling sound came from across the road. That was Lucky's so-called bird call, and although it didn't sound anything like a bird, his whistle was rather distinct and loud enough to hear. He had been hiding in one of the buildings and could move from building to building without being detected. His whistle indicated that something was wrong. When the birds' call came, you dropped what you were doing and took a defensive position.

"Em, did you hear that?"

"I did." He replied.

"I'll go up and have a look." Erin climbed the staircase to the second floor and made her way over to a window in a room facing the street.

Looking out, she could see two riders coming down the street. She couldn't make them out at first, Marauders maybe. Could be scouts, she thought to herself.

Marauding outlaws usually traveled in larger groups of six to ten; fewer of them would mean scouts. As they drew closer, she could tell they were not scouts. It was a bit of a relief.

Marauders were outlaws that would take their plunder by force rather than compromise by trading. Scavengers could not be trusted but were always open to trade. If they felt they got the better deal, they would often be willing to leave the area. There had been times when more than one group of scavengers would work in the same place, but rarely. They would often check back a few days later to retrace their route. Scavengers always thought themselves better than others; it was more common than not to re-scavenging an area after someone had just searched.

The two riders dismounted near the front of the building, unaware Erin and Emeric were inside. Erin quickly made her way back down the stairs; she already knew what would happen. The two Scavengers climbed off their horses, and while their hands were still on the saddle horn, Emeric walked out into the street with a gun in both hands.

"If you reach for your guns… you're dead!"

Both men paused while still holding on to their saddles. The rider closest to Emeric lowered his head, shook it, and said, "Took us by surprise, partner; didn't see you coming."

The men slowly turned around from their horses with their hands in the air just as Erin ran through the front door, guns ready.

"Looks like you got us, friends."

"Never been known as a friend to other Scavengers," Erin replied.

"Friendships come easy when you're on the wrong side of the gun," he paused briefly, then said, "now, come on, you wouldn't shoot a friend."

"I'd shoot my own brother if he tried to rob me." Emeric clearly stated.

"And I believe you would, mister."

"Who are you?" Erin asked.

"My name is Carlos."

"Carlos, what?"

"I'd rather not say."

"Might I remind you what side of the gun you're on?" Quipped Erin.

"Well, since you have the advantage, it's Carlos Smith."

"Excuse me, Carlos Smith?"

"Now you know why I didn't want to say. My mother was Spanish; my father was not." Pointing to the rider behind him, "This is my partner, Doc."

"My real name's Robert Galloway III," Carlos's partner quickly retorted without hesitation, "but everyone calls me Doc."

"We mean you no harm; we live by the Code," Carlos added.

"The Code," Emeric mumbled under his breath.

Erin just glanced over at him but said nothing.

"Can we at least put our arms down?" Carlos asked, "they're getting tired. You got us covered; we won't try anything."

Erin waved her gun at him, indicating they could put their arms down.

Carlos shook his hands a little. "It's getting close to sundown; we were looking for a place to shelter for the night. We spotted this little town from those hills off in the distance. Been up this way before, just not this far north and not past them hills," nodding to the south. "The Hills of Amidon, they're called. It's said that they're mysterious or something, named after this little town; they are the highest points in this area."

Erin glanced toward the hills with a sense of curiosity. "Why?"

"Why what?"

"Why are they mysterious?"

"Not quite sure. I met an old Wanderer a few years back. Said he traveled these parts…." Carlos gestured toward the hills in the distance with his arm, "lives east of here somewhere, around a river, I think, with his family." Carlos paused. "Something about an old myth or legend. Then the old man mumbled something. I wasn't sure, but it sounded like he said, the treasure of Amidon. Well, that's all he would say; it seemed to frighten him; he acted too like he shouldn't have said that. After that, our conversation ended."

Erin gestured, "come inside and out of the open." Inviting someone to join you wasn't safe, and Emeric gave her a skeptical look, but her curiosity was now inflamed.

Doc took the horses' reins and led them around the building and out of view. Erin went in first, then Carlos, then Emeric. Erin picked up a few chairs lying on the floor. Emeric positioned himself on the back edge of the bar, always at the ready. He didn't trust them; he didn't trust anyone, and in this position, he could watch the front and the back of the building.

"Thought we could spend the night and do some scavenging the next day," Carlos said as he sat down. Erin pulled up another chair and sat down across from him.

"Looks like we beat you to it."

"Looks like," Carlos retorted while glancing around the room, "any good finds yet?" He was curious. It was always a curiosity for Scavengers but something they never shared.

"Don't know... got interrupted. So, where are you heading from here?" Erin politely asked. She didn't want to sound rude, slightly indicating they couldn't stay…he didn't take the hint.

Doc walked through the front door; Emeric perked up, and everyone looked his way. "Hopefully, you'll let us spend the night, plan to head north in the morning as he pulled up a chair and sat down next to Carlos.

Ignoring Doc, Erin asked, "What's north?"

This was the furthest north Erin had been. Not many Scavengers wander north, especially later in the season when winter storms had been known to come on fast.

"Don't know." Erin replied, "Many of these little towns were inhabited longer than most cities; it took longer for famine and diseases to get out this far."

Doc was tired of the chit-chat and piped in, "got anything to trade?"

Erin was surprised the question didn't come sooner. Scavengers were loaners and didn't last long around others. His question meant it was time to do business and leave.

"Got an old .357 revolver I don't need."

Erin reached over to the Findings Bag on the floor, pulled out the gun, laid it on the table, and spun it. It wasn't loaded; she had checked when she first found it.

Doc leaned over and picked it up. "Cowboy up," he said, "Just like the old west, what ya all need for it?"

"Could use some 9's," referring to 9mm ammo.

Doc played with the gun, spinning it and acting like a cowboy.

Erin thought it was a little comical; he already looked like a cowboy of the old west, with a cowboy hat and long mustache.

Doc spoke up, "how many?"

"Three."

Carlos intervened, "three boxes, that's a little steep for that gun."

9mm ammo was the most used ammo making it the second most valuable trade, food being the first.

"OK." Erin injected. "I'll make you a fair trade. I've got two boxes of .357 ammo, and I'll throw in some fresh deer jerky. Picked it up from a Jerky Joe trader only three days back."

"Jerky sounds good; two boxes of ammo and an old western pistol - I'll go get the 9's." Doc got up from the table and headed for the door.

"By the way," Carlos remarked with a grin. "It's coming out of your supplies, and when you run out of 9s, you'll need to use that pistol."

Doc smiled, "Ya, well, you'll be singing a different tune when I'm not sharing my jerky."

Doc returned a couple of minutes later with the boxes of ammo. Erin got up, walked over to Emeric, opened his backpack, and pulled out a bag of jerky. She tossed it on the table, then reached back into the Findings Bag and pulled out the two boxes of .357 ammo she had found with the revolver.

Doc pulled it all in as if he had just won a poker game. "Nice trade!"

Erin sure thought it was.

"Well," Carlos paused. "We've enjoyed a stimulating conversation and made a fair trade today. All in all, I'd say it's been a good day."

Doc leaned back on his chair and waved his newfound toy in the air toward the door.

"There's an old house on the edge of town that's still intact. Mind if we shelter there for the night, we'll be on our way at first light?"

Erin glanced over at Emeric.

"Okay with me, it's a free country." Emeric flatly stated.

"Thank you, ma'am; it was a pleasure to meet you."

"And to do business," chimed in Doc.

Without a word, Carlos took off his hat, slightly bowed his head in respect, turned, and went out the door.

Erin realized he was pretty handsome and had dark hair; she had always liked men with dark hair. Erin was a dirty redhead, a redhead with blond highlights. Her hair was in a single plait today, tucked under a wide brim hat.

Carlos didn't have long hair like most men in the wild; he kept it short and well-groomed. These men weren't dirty with worn-out clothing;

they took care of themselves and their equipment. An indication to Erin that perhaps they were men of the Code.

The following day, they were gone, pulled out sometime in the night. Erin leaned against the door jamb, thinking of Carlos, looking out toward what he called the hills of Amidon when Lucky came out of the shadows from around the building. "Yep, they pulled out about three this morning. Good and quiet they were. I wouldn't have even known if one of the horses hadn't knickered; probably excited to be on the trail again."

"Thanks for staying back and keeping watch, Lucky," she said.

"It's my job to watch the back trail— besides, fives-a-crowd. Different, weren't they? Didn't get that uneasy feeling I usually get."

"It's the Code," she paused, "they said they live by the Code."

"Huh!" was Lucky's only response.

Erin gazed down the main street through town to the distant hills, deep in thought. When she turned to look back at Lucky, he was gone.

"I guess that means back to work." She turned to make her way back inside. Briefly pausing at the threshold, she glanced down the road… "Might like to see him again!"

CHAPTER 2

Erin headed for the room that had once been used as the bar's office. She picked up the equipment that she had stashed in the corner; this would be her second scan of this building. Making her way to the center of the room, Erin began setting up. She first set up the tripod mount. It had a connecting stem that stood straight up from the center. Erin would place the round orb onto the stem locking it in automatically. When she was finished and ready to remove the device, she would put both hands on it. The Orb would automatically detach for her to lift it off.

"Should have enough power for one more ferrous scan, then we can head back to base camp. We'll get back there by dark if all goes well."

Emeric didn't reply, but she knew he had heard her.

Their base camp was set up about 15 miles west of Amidon. They'd found a place in the hills, known as the Badlands, a strategic position. It gave them cover and the advantage point, high enough to watch the surrounding area. Most importantly, it had running water for them, their horses, and a place to charge their equipment batteries. A creek coming out of the hills usually had enough power to operate a small portable water turbine they brought with them. They also traveled with a mini solar panel for charging. The solar panel had less power taking longer to charge their equipment. However, the turbine could have all their gear charged within a couple of hours.

"Alright, I'm setting up for the next scan" She wasn't sure if she was talking to Emeric or herself. She picked up the control module by the handle. The control module had an eight-inch touchpad computer screen. She could point it in any direction, and the digitalized record would show details of what had been scanned.

Walking back into the main bar area, Erin touched the module's scan button, sat down, and waited for the orb to do its job. Just then, a thought came to her. She laid the module on the table, got up, and went to the carry case. She reached into one of the pockets and pulled out a manual. On the front, it read: *Tactical Operations Scanner TOS8.* At the bottom of the cover was a stamp in red ink that read, *Top Secret.*

The uniqueness of this scanner was its Infrared and thermal abilities. Erin had read that the Thermal scanner uses radiation to pick up heat signatures from the far end of the thermal spectrum. IR or infrared picks up lighter signatures from the higher end of the spectrum. The scanner also captures Electromagnetic radiation from objects that still hold a radioactive signature. Other capabilities of this scanner were GPS, EMP, NMR, GPR, *Ground Penetrating Radar*, and something called the Wave. It works basically like an X-ray or MRI machine. From what Erin understood, this scanner could read the signature of a person or any item that put off heat, radiation, magnetic field, and more. Most of these were difficult to understand, except for the electromagnetic scanner that reads ferrous and non-ferrous metals.

The five-minute timer she had preprogrammed began to chime. Erin reached over and touched the stop button; the scan was complete. Her thoughts wandered into the distant hills as she closed the book. *I'll have to read more on these later*; she said to herself, putting away the manual.

Erin took the custom-built carry case with her, walked over, and picked the computer module up from the table. When she got back into the office, she put the module on the floor and quickly packed up her Light Bender. She didn't want to take the time later to put it away. Besides, it was wise to do if they needed to get out in a hurry. Findings could be left behind; her Light Bender could not. She kept the carry case close to her as she moved the screen around the room.

The picture on the screen had several different settings. She was only familiar with a few of them. She could see the whole layout of a room and zoom up on other areas or set it to PMS; she wasn't about to tell the boys the computer had a PMS mode -- *Panoramic Material Scan*. She didn't know why but just thinking about telling them made her smile. With this setting, she could move the screen around the room, pointing and angling it in any position she wanted. She found this PMS setting was much easier to use. It also gave her a sense of direction, pointing her right to the spot she wanted.

Not many items in the room; an old desk had been moved across the floor and was up against the wall, and old file cabinets in the corner. One of the two cabinets had been bolted to the wall; the other was on its side with a few chairs scattered around it.

Erin pointed the screen to the ceiling and moved it around. It wasn't picking up any anomalies above the ceiling. She scanned it down the wall and targeted the module at the file cabinet standing against the wall. The module sounded a quiet beep when an anomaly came into view. An anomaly showed on the screen as a small cluster of lights. In PMS mode, items took on the shape they scanned. The side of the screen listed metals, minerals, and a few other things Erin didn't understand. The control module's handle allowed her to point the screen in any direction, pinpointing a specific location if she needed it.

Erin pointed the device toward the bottom of the file cabinet, still bolted to the wall, the angle was weird, but it looked like a bottle. The text on the side of the screen gave many different minerals, including glass and liquid. Erin set down her computer screen and pulled open the bottom drawer. It was empty. She looked on each drawer side and found the tabs to lift the drawer out. She set it aside when the drawer was out and took out her flashlight. Shinning it inside and around the floor, Erin found nothing under the drawer.

"I know what this is; you can't fool me. Just because I can't see you doesn't mean you're not there," Erin remarked, as if she were talking to the file cabinet.

The day before, it was a finger hole on the inside of the bar's countertop. It would be out of sight if this hidden compartment were anything like the bar. Erin stuck her head right into the drawer opening with her light and searched along the inside lip of the file base. Sure enough, a tiny hole was notched out of the wood floor corner, just large enough to get a tool into it. Erin climbed out, reached over to her carry case, pulled it closer, and unzipped a side pocket. Inside, she had tools to help dig things out from floors, walls, and furniture, anything that could be cracked open.

She pulled out a handled tool with a curved pick end on it. Erin climbed back into the cabinet with her flashlight, putting the curved edge of the pick inside the small hole, and slowly wedged up the floorboard. Once it was out, she put the wood inside the drawer sitting on the floor next to her. Retaking the flashlight, Erin peered into the hole under the cabinet. It was just what she thought it was; an unopened bottle of whiskey. She reached in and pulled it out.

"Well-well, I believe it's Lucky's lucky day," Erin said.

Of the three of them, Lucky was the only one who liked Whiskey. She stood up, brushed her pants off, and held up the bottle.

"Jack Daniels, well, how about that." She had to show Emeric; he was still standing near the front door when she walked back into the bar room.

"Look, Em, look what I found for Lucky!" she happily announced with a big grin.

"Great," Emeric replied with a smirky grin, "just what we don't need. Put it away; he's got eyes like a cat and in the back of his head, and don't give it to him until we get back to base camp."

Emeric turned and leaned back against the door jam. Looking around at the other buildings, he muttered, "he'll probably smell it before we even get back."

Erin put the bottle in the Findings Bag and went back to the office. As Erin reached down to pick up the computer screen, she stopped before grabbing it.

She thought to herself. *Why? Why was the only thing hidden in that hole a bottle of whiskey?*

Erin stood up straight and crossed her arms with her hand on her chin. A habit she often did when she was thinking. *Why would someone make such an elaborate hiding place to hide a bottle of whiskey?*

"Well, other than Lucky." She said out loud.

Erin got back down on her knees and looked around the hole with her flashlight. Nothing, nothing but dirt. Still not satisfied, Erin put her left hand into the hole and started feeling around. She pushed and scraped on the dirt walls. She then started moving around the dirt under the cabinet; she felt something. Sliding out, Erin grabbed her case and pulled out a small spade. Then reached into the hole and started pounding and punching the spade into the ground. Then click. She hit something that sounded like metal. Erin began to dig with the spade, pulling dirt out with her hand.

She had cleared out enough soil to expose a metal top; it had a handle. Erin pulled up on the handle with a hard tug, and the ground released the object.

Lifting it out from under the filing cabinet, Erin sat the box on the floor in front of her. It was an old, pale green army ammo box.

"Why didn't you show up on the scanner?"

Granted, she didn't know everything the Light Bender could do. She turned the computer toward her to look at the screen. The picture and text were no longer available; the scanner pointed in another direction.

"I'll have to pay more attention next time," she said.

She picked up the ammo box and headed back into the bar's seating area.

Erin walked right up to the bar, placed the ammo box on top, turned, and stood looking at Emeric with one hand on the ammo box and the other on her hip.

"Is that an ammo box?" Emrick questioned.

"It sure is."

"What's inside?"

"Don't know, haven't opened it yet. Thought, this is your kind of thing. Maybe you would like to open it?"

"Yea, I would; that'll be great!"

"Don't get too excited; it might cause you to smile."

"I am, on the inside."

As Emeric walked over to the bar counter, he asked, "where'd you find it?"

"It was buried in the ground, under the Whiskey bottle."

"Buried, really?"

"Don't keep me in suspense; open it."

Emeric pointed without looking, always thinking of safety, "watch the door for me."

"I will."

Emeric reached over and cracked the snap latch open. Having opened ammo boxes before, he put his left arm around the box, and with his hand holding it firm, he pulled up on the latch handle, and the lid popped open. He pulled the cover back and leaned over to look inside, pausing just long enough for Erin to get impatient.

"Come on, what is it!"

Emeric reached inside, pulled out a large item, and held it up. With her head cocked to one side and a tone of disappointed surprise, she retorted, "A key?"

"Look at the size of it… it took up most of the box!"

Emeric held the key up for a brief moment.

"Now, that's an odd shape for a handle. It looks like one of those old keys to a large metal lock or..." Emeric paused as he looked at Erin.

"Or what"? she said curiously.

"Or maybe to a large metal door. Oh, ya, now that would be cool."

"Yea, for you," anything else?"

Emeric reached inside, pulled out an old envelope, looked at it, and handed it to Erin. Erin took it with a bewildering look on her face. Emeric just shrugged his shoulders. He reached in and pulled out the last item.

"This is it, nothing else."

It was a small leather bag. Emeric opened it and dumped the contents into his hand.

"What! Are those gold bars?" Erin took one from Emeric's hand.

"Sure, looks like it," Emeric said.

"They must have been rough poured," Erin explained further.

"You know, poured into a rough handmade mold. It feels like it could be an ounce or more."

After a few minutes of staring, in what could be considered disbelief, Erin took the other two bars of gold from Emeric and put them into the leather pouch she wore around her waist.

"Let's wrap it up and head back."

She picked up the key and envelope off the bar top and put them into the Findings Bag. She went back into the office and put away the computer control module and all the tools she had removed earlier. Emeric had grabbed the Findings Bag and waited by the door for Erin. As the two emerged from the building, Lucky came around the corner, horses in tow.

"Any good finds," he asked.

"Tell ya on the road. Let's get moving."

Erin tied down the Findings Bag and tripod onto the packhorse, then the Light Bender onto her horse. She was the last to mount. They turned their horses and headed west, passing between the buildings and staying off the main road. It was still early morning, and crossing country meant hills, streams, fences, and stops to water the horses. If they kept their horses at an even gait, they could get to base camp an hour or two before dark.

The country they were passing through was called the Badlands. Scrubs along rocky buttes and dry creeks made up the vast countryside. Oak and pine trees grew on the hillsides, and in this enormous area of the Badlands, the hills and buttes sprang up between this open range. An enemy could appear from around a butte or within a deep crevice at any time.

Safety meant riding near the hills, staying close to the tree line to make a run for cover. Maintaining the horses at an even gait meant walking and trotting to keep them fresh; if an all-out run became crucial, a horse could run full out for about three miles. Their horses could do a mile or two more. The packhorse was, however, expendable. To save themselves and make it to cover, they could lose the packhorse and supplies, hoping those chasing them would discontinue the pursuit and settle instead for the spoils left behind. Shooting it out never ended well for either side. They kept water and jerky in their saddlebags for such a scenario.

A few miles into the ride, Lucky hollered up to Erin, "Well?"

"You want to know what we found?" Erin yelled back; she was in the lead. She reined in her horse and waited for Lucky to get beside her. They trotted side by side.

"Besides the gun and ammo, we traded to Carlos and Doc..."

Lucky interrupted, "on first name bases already, are we?"

Lucky had an unmistakable grin on his face. Erin ignored it.

"The other Scavengers," she corrected.

"We found a..," she paused, remembering what Emeric had said earlier about the Whiskey, "a key and about 3 oz's of gold in an old army box."

"Gold!... that's one of our best finds... Bingo!"

Lucky would put his hand in a fist, then swing his arm along his side every time he said Bingo. Erin didn't know why he would always say bingo or what it meant, and she never asked. Lucky put his horse into a trot and got out in front of them.

Emeric rode up and, while passing, looked at her with a sly grin on his face and said, "Bingo!" knowing it would irritate her. He knew how to push her buttons, and he took devious delight in doing so.

Erin's mind wandered; Carlos, Amidon, the key... *were any of these connected?* Just then, Lucky put his arm up with a fist. They all stopped and silently waited. Trusting Lucky's instincts had kept them alive and out of trouble more than once.

"Smoke!"

Both Emeric and Erin began sniffing the air.

"He's right; it smells like a campfire," Emeric replied quietly.

"How'd we not smell that?" Erin replied.

Erin and Emeric turned their horses in a circle while sniffing the air, trying to figure out where it was coming from.

"It's coming from the hills to the south." Lucky pointed.

"Ravagers?" Emeric asked.

"Hunters if they're Ravagers," Erin replied.

"Ravagers don't make campfires. They cold camp and eat raw meat." Lucky explained in a softer voice. It was his way of saying they needed to whisper more.

"Travelers?" Erin said lightly.

"If it is, they're lost or something," Emeric agreed. "Travelers often use the main roads or routes traveling from place to place. Some travelers are on the road to visit family or friends; or moving to a new location. They usually make camp in abandoned buildings and homes or along the road-but, rarely in the hills undercover."

"Could be Marauders or Scavengers," Lucky added.

"Only one way to find out," Erin said.

"You want to go in there? Why?" Emeric asked.

"Because, if they are Travelers or Wanderers, we can get news from where they've been and maybe some helpful information for this part of the country. Maybe they've traveled here before. If not, we leave them be and move on."

Erin was hoping for Wanderers; family clans, similar to Gypsies, made up of small spiritual family groups, consisting of a father and mother, daughters, sons, and often older children's husbands or wives. Some Wanderers have family members from other groups, taken in as extended family or by marriage. The Father is the leader and the spiritual guide. If a Father has passed, the oldest and wisest is chosen as the leader and becomes the Father.

Emeric looked over at Lucky and said, "Well, Lucky, let's go see if we can find ourselves some Wanderers!"

Lucky turned his pony and led them south.

CHAPTER 3

It was a mile before they reached the hills where the smoke was coming. The three rode into the tree line for cover, dismounted their horses, and tied them to the trees. Lucky gestured for them to stay put and, in a whisper, said, "I'll scout, wait here." Then he moved off into the hills.

Emeric and Erin soothed their horses to keep them quiet. About 30 minutes later, Lucky returned.

"It's those spiritual wanderers a little way into the hills—A few of them are outside the camp area as lookouts, with rifles. Never seen such a thing, and more clan members than I've ever seen traveling before."

"More? How much more?" Erin said to Lucky.

"Oh, about fourteen."

"That's more than twice the number they usually travel with," Emeric stated.

Lucky looked at Erin and smiled.

"He's growing up so fast. He knows his numbers; pretty soon, he'll be adding two plus two."

"Ok, stop, no time for wise guy stuff. Let's go introduce ourselves."

Erin climbed onto her horse and moved out. Emeric saddled up, and as he rode past Lucky, he leaned over from his saddle and said, "Keep that up, and it'll be three minus one."

Lucky smiled; he couldn't help a little bantering. For him, Emeric was an easy target.

Silently they rode into the hills toward the camp. Riding into any camp was risky. Wanderer or other, there were no exceptions. They all felt something wasn't right. Why so many of them? Why a lookout? What are they doing this far north, so close to winter? Emeric was right; the numbers didn't add up. When they got within hearing distance, Erin called out, "Hello, camp, can we come in?"

"Em?" Lucky quietly said.

"Yes, I see them."

Two men came in from the right with guns in hand. The third was on their left; he was one of the lookouts Lucky had seen earlier. Erin lifted her hands, "We mean no harm. We live by the Code; just wanting to talk, maybe learn any news of the world."

One of the men spoke up, "Please keep your hands free and come on in." He gestured with his gun to move forward, and the three moved toward the camp.

As they dismounted, a young man approached them – he seemed to be in charge. Erin asked, "Is your father home? We want to visit with him and pay our respects."

When Erin said she would like to pay their respects was a polite way of indicating she would pay or trade valuables for news and information.

"I am sorry for the added security. Raids from outlaws have increased. Father felt it was time we protect ourselves. Please, come with me."

Emeric and Lucky tied the horses to a nearby tree, and all three followed. He led them over to two campfires; an older man sat on a mat, his back against a rock.

"Father, here are your guests," said the young man. He then moved to the background.

Erin slowly walked over to the older man.

"Come closer, my child. Take my hand."

Erin would have made the customary and polite remark, thanking him for seeing them, but all she could do was take his hand and fall to one knee in front of him.

"Father, how old are you?" was all she could say. Emeric and Lucky were equally stunned.

He glanced over at Emeric and Lucky. "Young men, please come sit with me closer to the fire. I am an old man, and it gets more difficult every day for me to get up."

"I'm sorry to act this way," Erin said softly.

"Oh, no, don't be my child; you are surprised, I know. You must have many questions."

Erin released the older man's hands and glanced over at Emeric and Lucky. "My name is Erin. These are my partners, Emeric and Lucky."

"Nice to meet you. They call me Father Moses; I know, it's unusual; it's a biblical name. I've had many names through the years; I think they call me Moses because… I'm so old,"

Moses said louder while glancing over at the other fire.

"Now you hush about that, father." one of the older women hollered over.

Erin and the others chuckled. Father just waved a forgiving hand at her.

"I lived through the time of the destruction." He continued, "I escaped when I was…It's hard to remember, around 50, if I remember, just before the last bombs fell from the sky.

"That would make you then…."

"Yes, my child, over 100 years old."

The average lifespan in the new world was around fifty and near the same for women. Famine, disease, lack of medicine, and skilled doctors had taken their toll on humanity. If that didn't kill you, it was hard work, outlaws, Ravagers, or someone trying to survive. However, after the destruction, anyone would have killed for food to survive. Today, those that continue to do so are called Marauders or outlaws: no more than thieves and murderers.

Erin fell back off her knee and onto the ground.

"100? How is that even possible?"

"Well, I really can't say – but some would say clean living." He chuckled as if he was telling a joke to himself. He knew why he had lived a long, healthy life, but now was not the time.

He continued, "Others would say, by the grace of God or as some may refer to Him now as, the Creator. Right now, I can't tell you the reason why I've lived for so long. We live a simple, spiritual life. We keep to ourselves and never wander into the cities or townships. We trade where we can and, by the Creator's grace, are often spared from famine and plagues. To our grief, our losses have often come from Marauders and Ravagers. We mourn our loved ones we have lost and give thanks for the life we could share with them. We all must die; the key to life is giving thanks every day for the life we still have. That is the true blessing, not immortality. The Creator leads us on many paths. I look back and realize mine was a long one. In fact," Father Moses gestured toward Erin, "I believe He has led you here today."

"Oh, I don't know," Erin said with a hint of doubt.

"Enough with spiritual things; what can I do for you children?"

Erin felt like she had just woken from a dream. She shook it off. "Word, I mean news from your travels? Why are there so many of you here? Why are you so far north? Where are you heading?"

"Slow down, my child. We will discuss these things and more, but first, let's eat. The young men with you look famished."

Suddenly all three realized they hadn't eaten in a day, and the aroma from the food cooking on the other fire suddenly permeated their senses. Lucky grabbed his gut; it was growling.

Father gestured for the young man standing in the background to come over.

"This is my great-grandson, Dakota. Please, Dakota, would you have the others bring them food.

"Oh, no, father, we don't want to intrude further."

"My child, you are our guest and part of our known family; you are always welcome here."

"Known family, how are we known to you?" Erin was puzzled.

"You are known because you are from the earthly family. We are all connected as a family since the beginning of time. This new Code you choose to live by it's about family."

Two women about Erin's age came over and handed Emeric and Lucky plates of food and mugs filled with filtered water.

"These two lovely ladies are new members of our family; this is Gillette, and this is Sheridan. Thank you, ladies," Father Moses said.

The young ladies headed back to prepare more food.

"They have come to our family from the plains, this side of the Big Horns." Referred to the Big Horn Mountains of Eastern Wyoming.

"Okay, now I understand the names," Erin stated.

Lucky quietly leaned over to Erin and said, "I don't. What's with the names?"

Erin leaned closer to Lucky to explain. "Wanderers move from region to region. Never in one place very long. They teach their children to read and write, and since books are scarce, one of the ways they educated them was by reading signs on buildings and signs along the old roads and highways, anything that was still legible. For this reason, many would give their newborn children the name of the town or place they were born or had passed by while they traveled. Dakota, over there," Erin gestured, "is probably an exception; his parents chose a name for a territory rather than a town."

Lucky went back to eating his meal. Moments later, Gillette, one of the young ladies Father Moses had introduced, brought Erin food and drink.

Erin thanked her, then looked at Father Moses and said, "thank you, father, for this food." She paused. It felt as if she had just said a prayer.

Father Moses chuckled. He knew what she was thinking by the expression on her face. Both Emeric and Lucky had their mouths full, paying attention only to their food.

"What is this?" Lucky finally spoke. "The flavor, I can't tell, and the smoky taste. It looks like rabbit meat, but if my eyes were closed, I'd have no idea what it is."

"You'd have to ask the cooks; the wild herbs and spices they add can change the taste. Would you believe the women can take a rattlesnake and make it taste like chicken!"

There was a silent pause. Erin spit food as she began to laugh, then quickly covered her mouth. Lucky looked at her, then at Emeric, who had a pretty good grin. Suddenly Lucky got it.

"Oh, that was a joke. you got me on that one."

He just shook his head and continued to eat. For him, the food was much better than the joke.

"Father Moses, aren't you going to eat with us?

"Oh, no, I ate earlier. Getting too old. I can't eat too late, or I have trouble sleeping."

"Father Moses,"

"Yes, Emeric."

Emeric paused for a moment. He wasn't custom to being called by his full name. It felt as if Father Moses was referring to someone else.

"You can call me Em, father," Emeric said politely.

"Why, thank you, Emeric." Of course, Father Moses replied politely with no intention of calling him Em.

"You talked about family and said the Code has something to do with family; I don't understand."

"We are all family connected through time. Everything we do in our lives involves family. The Code that so many are trying to live by connects to family."

"I'm still not understanding."

"Let me put it another way for you. What is the Code? Tell me what it says to you; quote it to me."

"Um, OK, it's; Don't lie, steal, or kill; don't tolerate those that do, but instead, bring them to justice."

"Very well. Are you an educated man?"

"Me, educated? Oh, no. I can't even read well."

"See, Emeric, just because you can't read very well doesn't mean you're stupid. You are a smart man. I can tell this by how you act and how you talk."

Emeric sat up a little straighter and looked at Lucky with another big grin. Lucky had a disgusted look, then mumbled, *"Great, two grins, all within an hour."*

"So, Emeric!" Emeric looked over at Father Moses. "Do you have a family?"

Emeric glanced over at Lucky and Erin without them noticing,

"Ah, Yea."

"Good. Would you lie to your family?"

"Well, no, not really."

"Good. Would you steal from your family?"

"Oh, no, of course not!"

"Emeric!"

"Yes, Father Moses,"

"Would you kill your family?" Emeric paused. Suddenly he understood. An uneasy feeling came across them; they all understood. And they all knew the answer.

"In the Code, where you said '...bring them to justice,' what does that mean to you?"

"I guess, in the old days, it would be to kill them. I suppose in connection to family; I believe it would mean their punishment would teach them right from wrong."

"Again, everything we do in life, our rules, laws, and how we treat one another is because of our family connection." Father Moses sat quietly, giving them a few minutes to soak it all in.

They had finished eating, and the ladies came over and collected the plates and utensils. Once again, they thanked the ladies and told them how good it all was. Father Moses spoke up, "Well, how about some news from the outside world?"

"Yes, please," Erin replied, "we haven't been back to our home base in the Black Hills for months."

"Well, as you may know, the new cities are growing. Four townships west of the Big Horns banded together and became Codyville. I have not been there. When Sheridan came to us, she knew others that had been there. It's still far from Ravager territories, but they still fortified it. Sheridan told us they banded together to advance something called *Thermal Energy*. Education is still advancing in the new cities. There is more demand for books, especially those with knowledge of trades and technology. They are now bringing a fair-trade value at the markets."

Since the Technology wars, books had no interest; survival overshadowed education. Books became fuel, used to make fires and heat homes. Books were scarce. Erin was happy to hear this; her years of hoarding books while scavenging might pay off.

"We attended two trade markets over the summer. One was west of the Black Hills and the other closer to the Big Horns, known as Wyomingburg. The Markets were on the outskirts of the farming communities. It was the first time we had seen this. When entering the market, they would ask you to abide by the Code and, if raided, to defend the market at all costs. People would trade for goods and supplies, mostly for food and produce. Some hard goods were in high demand, and merchants from the new cities were looking for items that operate by electricity."

"Is there any news from the Black Hills since we've been gone?" asked Erin.

"All I've heard is that new mines have opened, and small communities continue to grow as the demand for Silver, Gold, and other metals increases. As for coal mining, communities west and southwest continue to expand as the new cities grow. More survivors are migrating north.

The desert wastelands of the south continue to get hotter, so crops and plant life continue to die. Rivers and other sources of water have dried up. Heat and starvation have taken more lives than expected."

"Will there be enough here, in our area, for a larger population to survive?" Emeric asked.

Father Moses glanced over at Emeric. "They do not get the snow and rain we do here in our western territories. If people are willing to work and organize, then yes, I believe so. It's not been easy to bring law and order to our area. We have the Code, many believe in it, but no one can enforce it. Ammunition and weapons are difficult to find. Outlaws take everything they can and horde it. They continue to grow in power because of this. Even in the new cities, few can defend themselves. They continue to live in fear." Father Moses paused. He looked over at Dakota standing in the background. "Has there been anything I've missed?"

"No, father, but they might be interested in the news and talk about the Ravagers... you believe the rumors have been confirmed."

Emeric looked back and forth from Father to Dakota,

"Talk? What kind of talk?"

"Stories of a young man that had escaped from the Ravagers." Father Moses said.

"I've always heard that no one ever escapes the Ravagers," Erin replied.

There have been some, including me."

"You, Father? A Ravager captive?

"Yes, for over two seasons. When captured, I negotiated to teach them better hunting, trapping, and hide tanning skills in exchange for my freedom, and they agreed. I was only buying time. I knew that no one ever left alive. You either died from hard labor, or they killed you. I knew they would never let me go. I helped them, hunted with them, and taught them skills until I found the opportunity to escape."

In genuine concern, Erin asked. "How did you escape?"

"I wanted them to get in the habit of me being around, so they would become complacent with me."

"Complacent? What is complacent," Lucky said with confusion.

Emeric spoke first, "It means they wouldn't worry about him running off; so, they might not always be watching him."

"And it worked; as they became complacent, they stopped watching me. Even if the hunters didn't know where I was or couldn't see me, I would still show up. The Ravagers never gave it a second thought. I was testing them."

Lucky was recreating the story in his mind, "So, how'd you do it?"

"In my hunting adventures with them, there were times when I would lead the way to a hunting area or someone else would. It was just random. In all the areas we had been in, I had kept my eyes open for a place to hide when they stopped watching me. And I found one. A hole in the ground led into a small cave. It was well hidden. They had passed it by many times. One time I was hiding in it as they passed by; I got out and caught up with them."

"Wait a minute; I don't understand. Why didn't you stay there if you were hiding?" Lucky blurted out.

"Because they would search for me maybe three or four days. If they came back to camp without me, someone would be accountable for it. They were Ravagers, but they were still human. No one would want to take the blame. So, I had to prepare. I needed enough food and water to outlast them in my hole and make the journey home. I would hoard food, wrap it up and drop it in the hole on our hunting trips. I took an extra-large water flask on one hunting trip and left it in the hole. That water flask could last me four days. I told them I had lost it. I got a good beating for that. I felt I had enough stored for ten days and built enough trust to carry another extra-large flask again. I was ready."

Erin was curious. "Weren't you afraid someone would tell of your plans?"

"No, I made sure no one suspected anything. In such a situation, survival is instinctive. I trusted no one. Someone would have turned me in, believing it would have given them a chance for survival. The day I planned to escape was like any other day; we moved out early, there were four hunters and myself; I took the lead and headed for my escape area. I slowly began to separate. When all four of them got ahead of me, I dropped into my hole. I thought they would kill each other when they couldn't find me, and at the time, I had hoped they would. They searched for four days and nights. They were tired and hungry. On the last day, they were near me, and I could barely hear them. They agreed they would all accept the blame and plan to head back. However, I knew that they would begin to blame each other when they got back. I got out of my hole that night, and by the next day, I was out of their territory."

"That was a great story," Lucky exclaimed.

"I learned a great deal about the Ravagers. However, the first year I was with them, a plague overtook them, not infecting any enslaved people, only the Ravagers. Some died, and others became ill. I didn't think of it at the time, but as I look back on it, I realize it must have been something in their blood or their diseased bodies. Something they may have passed on from one generation to another. Like me, this young man who had escaped told how the Ravagers had no children. He didn't know how long this had been going on and hadn't seen children in the two years he was with them. He claims he overheard them say: the women could not get pregnant."

"Wait a minute, Father, what are you saying?" Emeric said in shock, "these are the last ones?"

"Yes, blaming it on their diseased bodies; they believe this generation will be the last."

Once again, they all sat in silence.

"This is a confusing thought for me, father."

"How so, Erin?"

"I don't know how I should feel. Hearing this news, I am happy, but I also feel sad. The Ravagers have always been hated. They kill for no reason. They steal and destroy people's possessions and people's lives."

"That, Erin, is a normal emotion. It tells me you are human and understand right from wrong. That is why you believe in the Code."

"We all must die. Even the Ravagers." Father Moses continued. "But remember this; the key to life is giving thanks every day for what we're given. Life is a true blessing, and the key to life can unlock the door to a blessing or a curse. The Creator leads us on many paths, and sometimes our paths are unexpected. I do believe the Ravagers know they no longer belong in this world. Their path has come to an end. Know this; whatever path you choose, it can bring life or death… blessings or curses."

Erin stood up, having taken in more information in a few hours than she felt she had in her whole life. "Time to get a move on; Sun's going down."

"No, no, it's too late. The badlands are not a good country to be riding in at night. Too dangerous. Too many prairie-dog holes. Your horse could walk off a cliff. I am cautious; we now have a horse of our own." Father Moses pointed to the other side of the camp.

"There has been much that has been different here. I am old and cannot walk as well as I once could. We traded almost all the valuables we had for that horse. Now that I can ride, we travel faster than before."

"That was a wise and a fair-trade Father."

"Yes, I do believe it was. Tomorrow we head east. We have found a Winter camp along the big river—caves on the side of a hill. We can fish, hunt, and trap. We'll have many pelts to trade next season. Most of all, we are safe there. If you ever scavenge that far, follow the river west of the Dam. You are family."

"Thank you. I will always remember." The offer moved Erin.

"Now, make camp here and rest." Father looked over at Emeric and Lucky, "our morning meal is as good as the evening meal." After that, they needed no convincing.

Morning came fast. Last night still felt like a dream to Erin. It was the smell of breakfast that woke Emeric and Lucky. Before they could roll out of their bags, the Wanderers brought over food and drink. It was so much food they stuffed themselves. They wouldn't need to eat for the rest of the day. The Wanderers were packed and ready to move out. Father was standing next to his horse, getting ready to mount. Erin walked over to him.

"Father Moses, we would like to thank you and your family for taking us in. We want to give you a gift that we hope will help you and bring you many blessings."

Erin reached into the leather bag she carried around her hip, pulled out the two gold bars they had found, and handed them to Father Moses. She felt compelled to give Father Moses and his family something of great value. Erin knew the needs of others were greater than the needs of her own. Besides, the Light Bender had already made her wealthier than any other Scavenger.

"This is gold!" Father Moses loudly exclaimed. Everyone within hearing range turned their heads; all became silent.

Family members who had heard him say gold quickly came over to see. Many of them had never seen gold before and were excited to see it and touch it. Father Moses promptly handed them off to Dakota and took Erin by the arm.

"Where did you get this?" Father Moses softly said.

"I found it in Amidon," Erin replied with curiosity.

"Amidon!" Father Moses repeated. "Walk with me for a moment, so we can talk."

"Yes, Father."

"Erin, there are secrets in this world that one day you may discover. What you choose to do with those secrets will change the course of humanity. I do not know what you have been chosen for, but I believe you have been chosen. Our Creator has promised a new world, but our time is not His time. It is still possible that a new world is yet to come."

Erin thought this conversation was taking a strange turn but continued to listen.

"The key to life, Erin, will open more than just a door. What you find must be a secret. Trust only family. You know where their heart is. Many will kill to have those secrets…tell no one, trust no one!"

Father Moses turned Erin around and began walking back to his horse and his family, who had now crowded around Dakota.

"I've seen bars such as these before. They came from a handmade 2oz. Gold cast. It is worth more than we can provide and trade for over many seasons. Thank you for this blessing. We will use it wisely. Just as I believe, what you find will be used wisely."

"Thank you for your words of wisdom, Father." Erin paused, not understanding what those words meant, but she continued, "we are glad to be part of your family; I hope we will meet again."

"As do I. Farewell, my daughter."

"Farewell, Father."

Father Moses climbed onto his horse with assistance from two family members. When settled, he waved at Emeric and Lucky, who were preparing the horses, "Farewell, my sons, Emeric and Lucky." They made their farewells back and watched as the Wanderers moved on. It would be the first and last time they would ever see Father Moses.

Emeric turned to Lucky, "I have never experienced anything like this."

"Or the breakfast," Lucky added.

Erin walked over to her horse. "Are we set?"

"We are," Emeric replied. "What was that all about?" He pulled himself onto his horse and took the reins for the packhorse.

"I'll tell you later," Erin stated as she mounted her horse

However, Lucky hesitated and just stood there holding on to his saddle horn, looking at the ground.

"What is it?" Erin asked.

"By this time tomorrow, I'll be hungry, and I'm going to be missing those meals." Erin and Emeric nodded in agreement – as they rode for their camp.

CHAPTER 4

It was noon and hot. The horses were doing well. They were rested, grazed, and had plenty of water the day before. The three scavengers had been on the trail for about five hours, and their base camp was still a couple of miles ahead of them. They rode down an embankment and into a dry wash. It was the route to their camp. It was a strategic move when they chose their base camp. Once inside the wash, they couldn't be seen unless someone was standing on the upper edge.

The wash circled from the east to around the south side of the hills. As winter drew near, the Sun moved down the horizon. After a cold night's sleep, the party welcomed its warmth in the morning. Sundown in the evenings meant more light; it was always colder in the shadows.

When they reached the south side, they would ride out of the wash and through a ravine that cut between two high mounds, keeping them mostly out of sight. Rainwater would wash down from the hills, into the canyon ravine, then into the dry wash until the earth reclaimed it again, leaving only the sandy bottom.

It was common practice for Lucky to be in the lead. He always seemed to know something before it happened. And it did. Lucky suddenly stopped and gestured for them to dismount. They were only a quarter-mile from their camp. He handed his hat and reins to Emeric, ran around his horse, then straight up the wash embankment. When he got to the top, he slowly peeked over.

After peering over the embankment for about two minutes, he returned to Erin and Emeric. They all closed into each other no more than three inches apart so they could whisper to each other. "Marauders, six of them, north side of the hills, 1000 yards off. It looks like they're discussing something. Others are looking around like they heard something.

"Us?" whispered Erin.

"Probably"

"We haven't been talking that much."

"Certain words can carry a single sound pretty far in a breeze."

"What's the plan?" Emeric was ready.

"Slowly walk the horses not to raise any dust and keep them quiet if one nickers saddle up and make a run for the hills. If you make it without being discovered, keep watch; cold camp tonight. I will lead them off if I can. Don't expect me till around sunup."

Lucky grabbed his water sack, the pack of supplies from his saddlebag, and two extra ammo magazines, then headed on foot back in the direction they had come. Erin was suddenly thinking of the blessing they had in Lucky.

"Father Moses," Erin whispered to herself as if she were reciting a prayer. Sub-consciously, he had impacted her and her belief in the Code. Future events would, however, put this to the test.

They walked the horses slowly through the wash to the ravine. Off in the distance, they heard the call of a bird. Lucky was setting up a false trail for the outlaws. When they got to their exit, Erin and Emeric mounted their horse and rode out from the ravine to a high position in the hills.

They knew of a place where they could watch to the north undercover. While Emeric was tending to the horses, Erin made her way to a rocky cliff, allowing for a perfect defensive position and the best view in every direction except to the south. After Emeric had taken the saddles and packs off the horses, he grounded them in a nice grassy area. The horses would keep there with no desire to move for some time.

Emeric crawled up next to Erin, lying prone and looking over the cliff's edge with her.

"What's happening?"

"The outlaws have moved off to the north. They're following the wash."

"That would be Lucky. Leading them on a wild goose chase."

"I haven't spotted him at all. I hope he'll be alright."

"I'm sure he will; this isn't the first time he's outsmarted outlaws or anyone for that matter." Emeric always had something nice to say about Lucky when he wasn't around.

He was using the wash for cover as he led the outlaws north. When the wash no longer angled north, he climbed out, making his way undercover best he could. A mile further north in a deep ravine, Lucky found a mud hole tucked under an embankment the Sun never touched. He took off all his gear and rolled around in the mud. He remembered having done this when he was a child. It was a way to hide almost in the open without being spotted. He still enjoyed it, just as he did as a child. When finished, he took some mud and smeared it around his face and into his hair. If his head were sticking up, his hair would be like a dusty bush. If Emeric were with him right now, he would've said his hair hadn't changed much; Lucky smiled.

Climbing out of the ravine, he headed north again. He was moving further into the Badlands, leaving the openness of the range behind. The further he went, the more the landscape changed—deep ravines with trees and brush fed by natural springs – the Badlands teamed with life. At basecamp, they had spotted pronghorns and deer. During watch, he often saw coyotes in the evenings and even found a fox den not far from their camp.

The hills and cliffs were covered with orange soil and lined with dark coal deposits. Making his way further in, Lucky encountered wild turkeys, sage hens, and rabbits. Everything was lush and green. A beautiful landscape that should not be called Badlands. The Indians once called these places *maco sica* "lands bad."

Lucky planned to lure them into the hills to keep them confused. It seemed to be working. He left them a trail to follow; a broken branch, a rock overturned; he left a small campfire burning one time. They followed the smoke until the fire went out, then they lost sight of it. Further into the hills, Lucky began showing himself at brief intervals.

One might see him; then, he would be gone. He made a person's figure out of brush and branches and put it up on a distant hill. The Marauders ran their horses at full speed only to find that someone or something had tricked them.

After a long day of chasing something they couldn't see or find, the outlaws decided to make camp for the night. They found a nice little area with trees and a creek fed by natural springs. Lucky took advantage. The trees would give him concealment, and the sound of the flowing stream would help cover any unexpected sounds.

On the way to their camp, one of the Marauders stopped along a section of heavy brush. His horse began shaking its head up and down, nickered, and stomped its hoof. About 24 inches from that hoof laid Lucky in the low ground brush, undetected by anyone except the horse. The marauding outlaw became angry at the horse for stopping and making a fuss. He kicked the horse until it conceded, then took off at a run to catch up with the others. Lucky couldn't believe the horse would give him up. Then again, they were bred by Marauders. Lucky could have been caught if the rider had been more in tune with his horse.

When the camp settled down, Lucky made his way within listening range. Easy to do,

Marauders thought themselves so dangerous they didn't keep guard. After the drinking, many drifted off to sleep. Only a few continued in a discussion—the night's topic, whether to continue pursuit or move on. Most of them were tired of chasing what amounted to be nothing. Some thought it was a ghost. Lucky smiled, then decided to help them out. Later that night, when all had fallen asleep, the ghost would perform the skills everyone knew he had, but no one would see.

Early the following day, a disturbance among the men broke out. Several men had their money bags taken and wanted everyone to be searched to find out which of them had taken the money. Unknown to them, the missing money bags had been hidden in the saddlebags of their leader. Lucky began to move further away slowly. He could hear the men fighting and hollering, searching for their belongings. A couple of minutes later, he heard someone yell, 'Stryker! No!'; then gunshots. Lucky wasn't going to stick around to find out what happened; he headed south back to basecamp. His plan had worked.

Emeric and Erin cold camped that night; no fire, no hot coffee. Just jerky and water for their meals. They took turns keeping watch through the night. They would wake each other for the next watch about every four hours. Before sunrise, Emeric, who was last on the night watch, couldn't hold it any longer and left his post. When he got back to their base camp, Lucky had the fire burning and morning coffee brewing.

"I didn't see you sneak into camp; You're a mess. Did you fall into a mud hole? By the way, what took ya so long?"

Erin suddenly woke from Emeric's remarks and moved over by the campfire to warm up. Wiping the sleep from her eyes, she asked, "did you say, 'what took ya so long.' "Did Lucky go somewhere?"

She poured herself a mug of coffee from the fire and glanced over at Lucky, "Looks like you need a bath." Then gave him a wink and a smile.

They just sat there by the fire, enjoying its warmth and the company of friends.

Lucky put his coffee mug down and stood up. "Well, if you folks don't mind. I'm going to grab some clean clothes, head over to the creek, and clean up."

About 15 minutes later, Lucky showed back up at the campfire with clean clothes and hair combed.

"Don't you clean up nice," Erin said.

"Thanks." Lucky sat down, grabbed his coffee mug, and refilled it. He was shaking from the cold bath in the creek.

"I'm hungry," Lucky said, "got any breakfast to make?"

"Flat jacks and bacon sound good to anyone?" One of the many hidden skills Emeric had. No one would have guessed that this big gunslinger liked to cook.

"Still got any of that honey syrup?" Lucky asked. Realizing he, too, hadn't had anything but jerky in the last 24 hours.

"Found it," Emeric said as he walked over to the campfire with his supplies, opened the bacon wrap, and added five bacon pieces to the frypan. Two for Emeric and Lucky, Erin always preferred one.

"How is it you can make the best flapjacks in the territory?" Erin said with a hint of jealousy.

"It's partly in the pre-mix I make before we leave home. The other is making sure the stone or skillet is the right temperature."

Emeric had a particular way of mixing his batter. He took out about a third of the self-rising flour he made himself. Put it into a clear container with a lid. Adding about two cups of water and began shaking it. Looking at the mix, he could tell how thin or thick he wanted the flapjacks.

"Just about ready for the jacks."

Emeric flipped the bacon a couple of times, then moved them off to the corner of the skillet. He took out a little of his secret ingredient, bison tallow, from one of his containers and scraped it onto the edge of the pan. He could mix just enough of it with the bacon grease, so the flapjacks didn't stick. A minute later, he tossed in a couple of drops of water. The sizzle told him the temperature was just right, and when finished, the honey syrup added just the right sweetness to the jacks and bacon.

After breakfast, everyone sat back and sipped on coffee. Erin reached over and grabbed the Findings Bag. Inside, she grasped hold of the whiskey bottle…then paused. She had forgotten it was still in the bag. Glancing over at Emeric and knowing he might disapprove… she thought to herself; we've got one whole day here, and Lucky deserves it. Especially after taking care of the Marauders. With her hand still in the Findings Bag, Erin looked directly at Lucky.

"With all that happened yesterday, I forgot about this. I found you a little present." Erin pulled out the whiskey bottle and handed it to Lucky.

Lucky's mouth dropped open. "I can't believe it. It's a bottle of Jack! I haven't seen one of these old bottles since I was just a kid." Then the expression on his face changed. "I'm sorry, but I gave it up," and began to hand it back over to Erin.

Before she could take the bottle, Lucky quickly pulled it back and stood up. "What can I say. I lied." Lucky turned with a smile, then headed off for his morning nap.

"I can't believe you just did that." She shouted at him.

"By the way, thanks for the find," waving the bottle as he walked away.

The rest of the day was relaxing. Emeric tended to the horses. He gave them a good rub down and checked the packs and straps for wear and tear. He then filled all the water bottles and extra water sacks they kept on the packhorse using their water purification system.

Erin had connected the items that required charging to the mini water turbine she had set up in the creek. The electromagnetic pulse or EMP blasts that occurred over 50 years ago took out the country's electrical grids, communications, and transportation sectors just before the bombs fell. Many were permanently destroyed.

Harmless to humans, EMP bombs exploded in the atmosphere throughout the continent. Taking out communications permitted the nuclear bombs to hit their marks without hindrance from anti-missile technology. There are, however, things that EMP didn't affect; old cars, solar panels, and vintage electronic devices that used batteries. The equipment Erin and the others used were simple rechargeable devices. These types of items are commonly sold and exchanged at the markets. However, it was harder to come by solar panels and other charging devices that required the appropriate connection for a particular device.

After about three hours, Erin had everything charged. She put the turbine and devices into the packs they used for the packhorse. Lucky was scouting the hills, and Emeric was busy working on lunch.

Emeric was cleaning the potatoes when Erin walked up.

"We might have to do a little hunting when we leave—getting low on certain supplies besides meat," Emeric stated. "Lunch and supper tonight will be the last of our Pemmican. I'll cook it with the beef fat and fry up some of these wild potatoes Lucky scavenged for us. They'll make good potato fries."

"Sounds good. When did Lucky stop by?"

"About 30 minutes ago. He said he was heading up to the high point to scout. Said he'd be back in an hour or when lunch is ready; his exact words."

Lucky showed up just as Emeric pulled the food out of the cooking pots.

"Wow, you timed that well; glad you could make it," Erin said.

"Did you have any doubt?" Emeric replied. "He'd have to be tied up and gagged before he missed a meal!"

"Well, all I can say is… I'm glad to be here. I'd have hate for you to miss these wild potato fries."

Emeric looked over at Lucky, "Thanks, that's the nicest thing you've said to me all week."

Lucky only grinned back as he popped a potato fry into his mouth.

After everything was cleaned up, Emeric put on the coffee.

Erin grabbed the Findings Bag and brought it over to Emeric and Lucky, sitting drinking coffee. She pulled out the letter they had found a few days back, sat down, and took it out of the envelope.

"Forgot all about these until yesterday when I gave Lucky the whisky bottle." She reached back into the pack and pulled out the key, taking a moment to examine it.

"I still don't understand why it has this unusual bumpy shape."

Holding both the key and letter together, she read the opening sentence.

"If you are reading this letter, you are holding the key to life in your hands."

"Oh...kay, now that's a little weird." Erin felt a lump in her throat and swallowed.

"It's like… someone knew you would be holding the key." Lucky voiced with some humor as if no one else had caught on.

Erin quickly handed the key to Lucky, who started examining it.

Emeric's eyes lit up, "it's like I said before, it's a key to a big metal door."

"It's certainly big enough. Can't manage to think of anything else a key this large would fit." Pointing the key at Erin, he said, "go on, read more!"

Erin reopened the letter that had partly folded back. Taking a moment to scan the letter, she briefly looked up, "it's written as a rhyme and not a very good one, I might add."

If You Are Reading This Letter, You Are Holding The Key To Life In Your Hands.
From in the hills Of Amidon,, you will find a treasure From The Past For All Mankind.
Where You Found Me look through the glass Where the x lines up Begins Your Path.
From on the butte, This place All Alone, the key To Life into the stone view the path it In Time leads to What Is Shone. the eagle And The Directions Are in the rock, the key Of Life placed within Will Be No More.
Below the Eagle slot Found will unlock Here Too, Find the large entrance Without A door.
A Message, A beware, a warning For The Lesser.
how you use It, You Will Be Measured.
the Key To Life An Abundant treasure, will bring a curse of death or a life of joy and pleasure.

Lucky handed the key back over to Erin. She took the key, leaned back against a rock, and examined it.

"What was it that Father Moses said?"

"About what?" Emeric asked.

"About the key?"

Lucky jumped in; he recalled what Father Moses had told them earlier. 'The key to life; Father Moses said. Do you think there's any connection to what he said and the letter?"

"I don't know,' Erin said, "gives me goosebumps."

They all sat there, silently trying to recall what Father Moses said.

Emeric spoke up. "He said, 'remember… the key to life,' it has to do with blessings and unexpected paths."

"Yea, that's right, and something like the path you choose can bring life or death." Lucky wasn't sure if he had quoted it right.

"If you think about it, we take the wrong path out here; it could lead us right into Ravager territory."

"That's true," Emeric replied. "Life or death."

They were all staring at the key, then Erin spoke. "Remember when I gave Father Moses the gold bars, which by the way, were two ounces, not one."

Emeric and Lucky looked at each other with wide eyes.

"He pulled me away from everyone," Erin continued. "I think he didn't want anyone to hear, but he didn't make much sense."

"So, what did he say," Emeric asked.

"Well... first, he asked where I had got it. I told him I found it in Amidon. Then he talked about secrets. He said that there are secrets in the world, and what I choose to do with those secrets will change... I don't know... my course or the world's course."

"What secrets? We don't have any secrets...do we?" Lucky asked.

"Is that all he said?" Emeric asked.

"I'm thinking, Em! Something about the key...oh, he said, the key to life will open more than just doors. And that I shouldn't trust anyone except my family and that people or someone would kill to get my secrets – so I shouldn't tell anyone. Actually; he said, 'tell no one.'"

"And now you told us," Emeric said with a grin.

"He said except family, and you two are my only family," Erin replied.

"Well, still, that's a lot to take in."

"I thought it was just a metaphor," Erin added.

"A metaphor of what?" Emeric asked.

"Of my life."

"I don't know about you guys," Lucky replied. "But I think this has to do with the key Erin found. After all the references to the key in the letter and Father Moses and about a treasure - this stuff is secret or should be kept as a secret…right?"

"What stuff is secret?" Emeric asked.

"The stuff Erin found. The letter, the key – it's a map of sorts…a treasure map!"

Everyone sat in silence, thinking if what Erin had found was a map. A map of clues. Then Erin spoke up.

"So, what do you think about the letter?"

Lucky quickly spoke up, "don't rhyme very good."

Erin smiled, glancing down at the letter. "No, what I mean is, what do you want to do about it? Do you think this treasure stuff is real? Or are we just wasting our time chasing something that doesn't exist?"

"I've never really taken stock into myths or legends." Emeric expressed, "we did find the letter and a key. I am curious to find out about the key. That, and there's been a lot of references to it since we found it. Maybe there is something to it."

Emeric got up and started pacing. Lucky took out his pocket knife and started picking his teeth clean. A habit of many men who wandered in the wild and something he did when he was thinking.

"If we go searching for this treasure, we'll need to go home first and resupply." Lucky picked up a twig and began etching a line on the ground. "Hard to say how long we might be gone or what tools we might need."

"Lucky, you'd chase down a rattlesnake if you thought it had a gold tooth," Erin replied.

Lucky just looked up and smiled. "Never stood by one long enough to find out," Lucky shot back, still smiling.

"There you go again, getting all his hopes up," Emeric taunted. He turned and headed down to the creek with a funny smirk on his face.

Lucky glance over at Erin, "he had a grin on his face, didn't he? Great, too early for that to be starting."

The rest of the day was easy. Emeric went for a walk near the creek. It was a beautiful calm day. It was cool out, yet the Sun felt warm. The song of birds blended with the quiet rippling of the water. The grass was green, and the trees were changing to fall colors. After years of heartache and despair, as a young man, every day was a fight to survive… yet he was at peace in this beautiful place.

"Well, I found a nice comfortable place to rest," Lucky said. "If I fall asleep, holler at me in about an hour. If I take too long a nap, I won't sleep tonight – and you know what that means for the next day."

"Oh, I do," Erin replied.

She knew too well that Lucky slept no more than five hours a night and always took the early morning watch. If he didn't sleep at all, he'd be hell to deal with the next day; crabby, cranky, and pouty.

Morning came too early for everyone. Either their day of rest was too much or not enough. After a simple breakfast and coffee, Erin went around the backside of some large boulders to where they had hidden their stash of supplies. Weeks earlier, they dug a hole underneath some boulders just large enough to hide their supplies. She moved a couple of medium-size rocks and started collecting the supplies. If anyone needed something from their supply stash, they always ensured everything was wrapped well before replacing it.

About 20 minutes later, and having made two trips to the stash, Emeric walked over with the packhorse.

"I'm going to go collect the other horses and get them saddled up; you got this?"

"I do," Erin replied.

Emeric turned and headed down the hill to where he left the horses grazing. Erin got the packhorse loaded and ready to go. By the time Emeric got back with the horses, an hour more had passed.

"Where's Lucky?" Emeric asked.

"Right here, behind you."

Emeric jumped a little. "Don't do that. One of these days, I'm going to shoot you for sneaking up on me."

"Why, you should know it's me. I'm the only one that can sneak up on you."

"Where were you?" Emeric asked.

"Climbed to the top of the boulders as high as I could to have a look around and check our back trail."

"You spot anything?" Erin asked.

"Nope, nothing to worry about. I thought maybe I saw some dust, 10 or 20 miles to the southeast. Hard to tell. It could've been wind pushing the dust. However, it is the end of the season; it could be a herd slowly moving south."

"If it is bison, it could be a chance for some meat and fat. I'm getting low on Tallow, and bison fat is the best." Emeric paused. "Either way, good to be aware of it. You know me - hate to be surprised," he glared at Lucky.

About 10 minutes later, the trio headed down the ravine on the south side and into the wash. The wash would take them another mile south. There they would climb out of it and make for the North-south Trail.

This trail ran north and south of the Black Hills, mostly staying off the old highways. Both sections often kept to the hills and wilderness areas, partly for the cover of safety and making camp, the other for hunting and trapping.

They would pick up the trail near the town of Bowman that intersected these routes. Sometimes called the Bowman trail due to the trail sometimes following alongside the old highway. Long rides on the pavement were hard on the horse's feet and legs. Some trails followed paved roads; for this reason, others did not.

Outside of Bowman, the path would veer off to the northwest. They say the North-west trail ends at the Great North River, once called the Yellowstone. Erin and her partners had never been that far north. Amidon was the farthest north they'd gone in two years of scavenging.

Lucky was already getting bored with the ride. He looked over at Emeric, "so, you don't like to be surprised?"

"Nope," was Emeric's reply.

"Really?" Lucky just starred at Emeric.

Lucky was a casual rider, one hand on his hip, the other on the saddle horn, the reins between his fingers.

"Not even on your birthday?"

"Nope, I can't; I don't have a birthday."

"Yep, know how you feel, me neither."

"You two act like a couple of lonely cows waiting for the slaughter," Erin pleaded, "please, give my ears some rest!"

Everyone chuckled except Emeric. It was his second grin for the day, and it was still morning, and, of course, Lucky noticed it too.

CHAPTER 5

It was over 20 miles before they would reach the North-south tail, a full day's ride.

They decided not to push it; none felt like they had much sleep the night before. Once on the trail, if they kept the horses at a steady pace, they might make 40 miles per day, putting them home in three or four days.

About ten miles north of the trail was a small lake. A quiet secluded lake in the hills surrounded by pine trees and wild raspberries. Berries were pleasant to chew on in the evening while relaxing after a delicious trout meal around the campfire.

They camped at this same lake a few weeks before. Lucky did some fishing and was looking forward to doing some more. The trout would be great for dinner, and if he got up early enough, he might catch some more for breakfast; rolled in some of Emeric's homemade batter… his mouth began to water.

"Are we there yet?" Lucky asked again.

"Would you stop that? You'd been asking for the last couple of hours," Erin complained.

"Well, are you sure we're going the right way? The lake wasn't on this…."

"Really? Would you stop?

The word "Trail" rolled off Lucky's tongue.

Just then, they heard gunfire. Reining in the horses, they waited. Then, more gunfire. Emeric and lucky glanced down at their horse's ears and said in unison... "to the southeast!"

"Damn," Lucky said, "I knew it; we've been riding in the wrong direction."

"Wrong direction for what?" Emeric said, "relaxing by the lake or running into trouble?"

"Too late for any of that now," Lucky complained, "we'd better see if someone needs help!".

Erin took the lead and headed southeast, a hilly area with large pine trees. Lucky had thought they should have been on the east side of these hills. They picked up the trail too early, meaning they were too far west; they should have connected with the trail after their stay at the lake. He wished now he had said something earlier.

Ten minutes later, they were winding their way through pine trees, boulders, and brush. While working their way around the edge of a hill, another gunshot rang out—about a minute later, another.

"Could be trying to shoot someone moving around, or someone's pinned down," Lucky said.

"Could be taking pot shots to keep someone pinned down while others outflank them," Emeric added.

Erin glanced over at Lucky, "want to have a look?"

"That's why you pay me the big bucks."

"Please be careful. If you die, Emeric's getting your big bucks."

"Now she tries to be funny," directing his comment to Emeric as he rode off into the trees.

Lucky climbed the hill as far as his horse would carry him, then loosely tied her to a tree. He brought his 9mm Smith & Wesson in a shoulder-strapped holster centered over his heart. He liked this location. If he needed it fast, he could reach it from any position. It didn't matter if he was on his horse, crawling on the ground, or having to hide in a small, tight place; he could reach it. Extra ammo magazines he kept on a side belt; he carried six. Erin thought it was too many; Emeric said it wasn't enough.

Lucky made his way up the hill and around some boulders. He wanted to reach a high position to scout the area while trying not to be seen. As he came around a boulder high up on the hill, he spotted someone behind a rock with a rifle pointing down into the ravine. He quickly and silently stepped back behind the boulder. Damn again! he thought to himself. Lucky didn't swear very much, but today just happened to be that day. Marauders, he almost said out loud. He had a feeling it would be that, and the distinct tat markings were a sure giveaway.

Get close enough, and you won't forget the tattoo markings of a Marauder. So that other marauders don't shoot each other in the back, they tattooed two guns in a crossbones pattern on the back of their necks. It was the first thing Lucky spotted. Other tats were usually horrifying scenes of death and destruction, an accurate revelation of the apocalyptic past.

Lucky moved around the backside of the boulder. He didn't want to kill him but needed to take him out; he needed that position, and one less Marauder, was one less they'd have to deal with. the elements of surprise were always helpful. If no one is expecting something, they only pay attention to what is at hand. In this case, the Marauder put all of his attention into the situation below him. Lucky turned his rifle around, gunstock out. He would use it to knock the Marauder out. He was sure this was the guy taking pot shots keeping, whoever pinned down; he waited for the right moment.

The Marauder fired his rifle. The loud crack of the gun would deafen the shooter long enough for Lucky to get behind without him knowing. Lucky jumped out from behind the boulder, gun butt in the air, ready to strike, then paused. The outlaw was already collapsed over the rocks, dead. Lucky quickly looked to the right, the only direction someone could have come from, and there, for just a brief moment, stood an Indian? Then they were gone. Or, she was gone?

Lucky had no time to think about it now, but later, he would remember the scene. An Indian in beaded leather standing next to a boulder. A large knife with blood on it in one hand, a rifle in the other. The Indian wore a gun and leather holster around the waist; an ammo belt slung around the shoulder. The long dark hair was pulled back and tied. Smeared on the face, colors of red and black, and the look in the eyes; were of confidence and determination.

Lucky leaned his rifle against the large rock, grabbed the man's jacket at the shoulder, and turned him; his throat was cut, and his rifle was gone. Lucky turned and looked into the trees spotting what he needed, a downed branch. Taking it and a large stone, Lucky propped the dead man's head on the rock, laid the long tree branch beside him, and tucked it up under his arm as if he were holding a rifle, then turned the man's head to lean onto the tree branch as if he was looking down the barrel of the gun.

If his raiding partners knew where he was, and he was sure they did, they would be looking up from time to time. Lucky laid down on the rock next to the dead man, pointed his rifle above the tree line, and fired. If someone were looking up, they might see the flash; if not. The sound of another shot would convince his associates he was still there, giving Lucky, and whoever the Indian was, more time.

Emeric and Erin rode further into the trees and found a spot around some boulders where the horses would be out of the way and not easily found. They loosely tied up the horses allowing them to feed on the grasses. Then, Erin unbuckled the straps on the saddle connected to the Light Bender's carry case and put the case down. Reaching into a saddlebag, she pulled out a small tear-drop-shaped, one-strap backpack she could swing around her back then twist around to the front.

Emeric watched her take the Light Bender out of the carry case. He didn't think too much about it; she never let it out of her sight. She unzipped the pack's main compartment and placed the Light Bender inside. She took the control module out, unscrewed the attached handle, and put them into the backpack with the Light Bender. She pulled out two boxes of 9's from the saddlebag and put them into her pack's front zipper compartment. She slipped the backpack over her head and onto her back.

"Ok, I'm ready to go," she said to Emeric.

Emeric walked over. He'd taken out his 9mm Hi-Tec semi-auto rifle. He had two handguns, both 9's; one on the side hip, the other in a shoulder holster. He had a unique shoulder holster that carried four extralong 30-round magazines. He had taken two and taped them together back-to-back; the other two were the same. He could pull the magazine from the rifle, flip it over, and load the other in less than four seconds when one was empty. If Emeric was coming up against Marauders, he needed plenty of firepower.

"Check your sidearm," he said to Erin.

Knowing the number of rounds in the magazine during a firefight was essential. Erin pulled her 9mm Smith and Wesson out of her holster; Lucky and she carried the same model handgun. It was convenient for them. If one ran out of ammo, one could pass their matching magazine over.

She pulled back the slide just enough to see one round was loaded, then released the magazine and checked the number of bullets remaining.

"Seven in the clip, one in the chamber," she said to Emeric.

"Let's move out then. And it's not a clip. It's a magazine."

Erin just shook her head.

Rather than going up into the hills, they made their way along the tree line that skirted them. If they could make their way around this first hill and into the valley where the gunfire seemed to have come from would give them the advantage. Whoever was in these hills would have come into the valley on foot or by horse. If you were on the trail or just making your way across the country, you would camp near water and in the cover of trees.

If someone wanted to take a camper by surprise, then they would leave the horses in the valley or on the edge of it and sneak up through the hills, or as they say, 'take the high ground to pin someone down,' making it difficult if not impossible to escape.

"Hold up," Emeric dropped down into a draw.

Erin noticed it too. If this little draw still had fresh dirt or mud, they could get an estimated number of riders.

"Looks like about six riders," Emeric said when he returned.

"Then, I guess we're following them."

A soft nicker was heard when they got a couple of hundred yards into the tree line. They had guessed it right. Horses were tied up here in the valley while the outlaws or whoever continued on foot. Emeric gave Erin the signal to move around to the north and up the hill to create a distraction, a tactical plan they had used more than once before, and something they learned well from Lucky; the element of surprise.

Erin went up the hill. Here she would have the high ground and watch while she made a distraction. Emeric had made his way in close enough to see four horses through the trees and one person to watch the horses.

The plan was to get the guard to move toward Erin. He wasn't sure if she could see him; he just had to wait on her to start the distraction, and hopefully not too soon. Emeric knelt behind a group of pine trees and scrubs. A few minutes later, rustling noises and the whining of an injured animal could be heard up the hill. Emeric wrinkled his nose and said to himself, *poor, sick, animal...sounds terrible.*

Peeking through the trees and scrubs, he could see the guard turn and look up the hill. The sound stopped, and the guard turned back around after a brief pause. Suddenly there was a loud crack; an injured yell sounded. Emeric jumped a little. Whatever it was, it scared both of them. The guard jumped to his feet and grabbed his rifle. Then the rustling and whining started again; the guard moved toward it. When the whining became louder, the guard lifted his rifle ready and slowly moved past Emeric. Emeric moved around the trees and got up behind the guard.

"Hey!" he shouted. The guard jumped and turned off-balance as Emeric's fist made contact with the man's face. The rifle flew as he spun a complete 360, landing right on his back, out cold.

Emeric was dragging the man back into the trees to tie and gag him when Erin came down.

"Oh, Great! Marauders. Was he watching the horses?"

"Yep, usually the one who watches the horses is called the Lesser; less kills than the others. See the tattooed slash marks on his forearm?" Emeric lifted the man's arm and turned it. "Usually, the slash marks circle the forearm. And when the circle is complete, they can move up in rank, and a new row starts. This young man has only five; he has five more to go before he can move up."

"Move up to what?" Erin said.

"I don't know, cook maybe." Emeric thought he was trying to be funny, but Erin wasn't laughing.

"That's five people dead and five more just for a rank?"

Emeric had no reply, no way to say what they already knew. The strongest survived. It had always been; kill or be killed.

"While I tie him up and gag him, go through their supplies and bags and grab any ammo or guns you can find. If any of them survive, it'll be long before they harm someone else.

"And Oh, ya, I'm sure I don't have to remind you, be careful around their horses; they bite; mean, just like their owners," Emeric added.

Erin had gathered up all the handguns and ammo she could find and put them into a saddlebag found on the ground.

Emeric returned with two long thin twigs in his hands and handed one to Erin.

"What's this for?"

"Quieter than the sound of gunfire," Emeric replied.

"Alright then, let's turn them loose."

They unbuckled all the saddles, let them drop to the ground, removed the bit and reins, and began switching the horses' rears with long twigs. The horses jumped and kicked, then suddenly, as if they sensed their deliverance to freedom, turned and made for the tree line and open plains. Emeric knew full well they would eventually return to their home. But for a while, the marauding outlaws would be without horses.

Erin tossed the saddlebag over her shoulder, "good work, let's stash this bag and see if we can help Lucky or whoever."

Both followed the horses toward the tree line to hide the saddlebag of guns and ammo.

"That was some scary sound you made up on the hill; the Marauder and I both jumped," whispered Emeric as they moved through the trees.

"It wasn't me; it scared me so much. I think I peed myself a little. I'd never heard anything like that before. Came from further up the hill."

"Well, whatever it was, it helped."

They stashed the saddlebag near the edge of the tree line just in case any of the Marauders showed up. Then made their way up into the hills avoiding the outlaw's camp

About a mile into the hills, they heard Lucky's bird call. Both Emeric and Erin stopped. To keep moving meant they might lose him. Although Erin and Emeric couldn't see him, they were sure Lucky knew where they were, so they stayed put. About 10 minutes later, Lucky came through the woods.

"It's me, don't shoot the messenger."

"Very funny," Erin replied.

"We found their horse camp, disabled the guard, tied him up in the trees, hid their extra guns and ammo, then freed the horses."

"What, those mean little fillies; you're telling me they actually left?" Lucky said.

"They'd probably bite you if they heard you call them that," Emeric joked. "Took them a minute or two - but they figured it out."

"Alright, boys, enough playtime; we need to find whoever the Marauders are after and help them."

"Too late," Lucky replied somewhat sheepishly.

"Why?"

"Already dead. Sorry, I didn't want to say anything right away. The Marauders must have gotten them when we first heard the shooting. I found their camp. There were three men, possibly Scavengers or travelers; it looked like the firefight didn't take long. Nothing was taken or disturbed; The Marauders didn't destroy the camp or take anything. It was like they were just interrupted."

"Interrupted by what?" Emeric asked.

"Interrupted by us," a voice came from behind them.

All three spun on their feet with guns in hand.

"Indians," Lucky said.

"And... again, too late," Emeric said to Lucky.

Two Indians were standing in the clearing. The Indian in front raised his hands, "don't shoot; we mean you no harm."

"All right," Erin said, "what are you doing here?" It was the only thing she could think to say.

"We are here to help you; you are here to help us... we were unable to help the men that are killed," replied one of the Indians.

"I guess you already have us surrounded since we didn't even know you were here," Erin glanced around.

"I knew they were here!" Lucky abruptly announced.

"And again, too late," Emeric repeated.

Erin holstered her gun, and the others followed suit.

"Who are you, and what happened here?" Erin asked.

The first Indian walked over to them; the other stayed where he was.

"I am Two-Kettles, a very great descendent of a great peace chef of another time. To my warriors, I am called Scarred Face."

"I can see why," whispered Lucky to Erin.

"Hush," she said.

"I am sorry if my face frightens you. It was the work of Marauders when I was a young warrior. It took a year for me to heal. Now all Marauders are enemies. We are the warriors who hunt them. We cannot live in peace until they are gone."

"I agree with you, chief Two-Kettles," Emeric said. "Oh, I'm sorry, may I call you a chief? If Two-Kettles, your ancient grandfather, was a chief, I would assume you are too."

"Yes, I am. And you may call me Chief or Two-Kettles."

"Chief Two-Kettles," Erin said. "We should be leaving this place; the rest of the Marauders will be back for their horses and find them gone."

"Yes, we know the horses are gone, and so are the Marauders."

He waved his hand without looking away; an Indian came out of the trees with all their horses in tow.

"We put the personal belonging of the dead men into a sack and tied it onto your packhorse. We did this after your man," gesturing toward Lucky, "left the dead men's camp."

"That would be Lucky, our scout," Erin pointed over to Lucky.

"Yes, he is lucky and a good scout.

Lucky began to lift his arm, finger extended to correct the chief - Emeric grabbed his arm, slowly pulled it down, and whispered, "Don't."

"Thank you for bringing their belongings to us. If we can, we will notify their families," Erin said.

"Yes, it is good to know."

"Can we help you bury the dead men?"

"No, we have taken care of it."

"OK... well, we left one of the Marauders tied up in the trees, and we hid all the guns and ammo in a saddlebag near the tree line; you are welcome to them."

"Yes, thank you, we have found the guns and the man you left in the trees."

Erin knew they needed the guns and ammo more than they did, and she knew better than to ask about the Marauder.

"One of my best warriors didn't know your man was there in the cliffs," pointing to a high ridge, "until he came out of his hiding place. This is Yalonda."

No one had noticed her standing next to the chief until he motioned to her.

"I knew it was a girl!" Lucky whispered under his breath.

"Yalonda in our language means 'Little flowers of violet.' She is called Yalonda Little Flower."

As tall as her chief, Erin suspected Yalonda was about her age, not soft and delicate as violet flowers, but rather firm and trail hardened, yet still very beautiful. For a fleeting moment, Erin thought, *she would be a worthy opponent even for Emeric.* Emeric, however, couldn't take his eyes off of her.

"She is one of many warriors that are not men. After the ancient fires fell from the sky, only a few were left. The old tribes and the old ways are gone; now all are warriors."

"That we can agree on," Emeric replied, his eyes still on Yalonda.

"You are good people." She spoke. "You came on your own to help others in need, and you knew not who you were helping."

Yalonda turned her head and looked directly at Emeric. "You came because of what you call the Code? Is this true?"

Emeric felt a little discomfort. Yalonda had directed the question to him, and he wasn't exactly sure how to answer.

"Yes, I suppose it is," was all he could say while thinking; *why does everyone direct those questions to me?*

"I saw you, riding from afar, and you did not hesitate. When the dead men were found, your man did not take from them. When you found the evil men's horses, you did not kill the man holding them; you did not take from their horses. When we brought you their belongings, it was kind of you to say you would find their families. With respect to our needs, you offered us the extra weapons, not keeping them for yourself. As I am told, this is the way of the Code. Is it not?"

"It is," Emeric replied.

"Your people and our people, we share a common enemy, and by helping others in need, we, together, share the code," Erin added.

"Coming to the need of others, you have helped us in our time. Because of this, you are now part of the *Mahpe Chigakwa* people. These are Dakota words that mean 'Water Near the Forest.' Since the earth has lost its people, no one can speak the native languages, only scattered words by a scattered people. If you find more of our people, tell them you are *Sidanelvhi* of Two-Kettles and Yalonda. You will be safe; they will help you with any need. Sidanelvhi is old Cherokee; we consider you as part of our extended family."

"We are honored to be family," Emeric said.

Erin and Lucky replied the same.

"Now, before you go. I must finish my task; a prophecy is foretold. Three nights past the first full moon, I received a vision. Three riders, one a woman, were on a quest and could not be delayed. Their destiny was before them, and they could not waiver from it, for evil men followed, men who harm. Deep within the earth, darkness came against them. They did not despair; they fought the darkness, for light was with them."

All three stood in silence, motionless. None had ever heard a prophecy or been part of one, yet, this one seemed to fit.

"Yalonda, I'm sorry, I don't know what to say or what it means?" Erin said with empathy.

"It means that if you are not on the chosen quest, you must turn back and follow it without delay. Evil men are on the same path; you must complete the quest before they do. I saw an old man, an old warrior. When you find him, he will give you spiritual guidance. That's all I have seen.

"What harm? What path? What old man?" Erin asked in confusion. No other words of help came.

"I have seen no more. If this quest is yours, then you must follow my words. Upon my request, we have supplied your packs with supplies and food. Remember, without delay."

Yalonda had nothing more to say. She quickly turned and disappeared back into the forest.

"Chief Two-Kettles," Erin said, "thank you for the supplies. It is a great honor to be part of your family, but we must move on. My grandfather would always say, 'May your path be as true as an arrow and straight as a soldier's sword."

"Interesting thought, this I will remember. Your grandfather was a wise man. It means one thing but says another."

Erin had a puzzled look on her face.

"Our path is true, but it is never straight - just like most soldiers' swords were curved, not straight."

"Wow, I never thought of it that way!" Erin replied.

"Certainly, describes our path," Lucky said.

Emeric agreed. "I think we still have much to learn."

Having got caught up in the conversation, Erin remarked, "It's time for us to go."

"Thank you, Chief Two-Kettles," Erin said as she turned back to the Chief, but just as mysteriously as he appeared, he was gone.

CHAPTER 6

The day was getting late; dark clouds began to fill the sky.

"We should put on a few more miles and make camp early. This cool breeze is bringing rain; I can smell it." Emeric said.

They all climbed onto their horses as if in agreement. Emeric took the reins of the packhorse, and they made their way out of the forest. Just as they cleared the tree line, the three riders came to a stop. Lucky was the first to speak.

"If we turn north and camp at the northern edge of the forest, we could make Amidon by noon tomorrow."

"As usual, you never turn down the opportunity for adventure, even if it is dangerous," Erin said.

"Well, one advantage, we now know, thanks to Yalonda, we'll need to watch our back trail," Emeric replied.

"Probably even more now than before – let's go!" Erin turned her horse, and the others followed.

After about three miles, the group found a nice alcove in a rock wall and far enough within the tree line that others couldn't easily see them. It would rain through the night, and they wanted the best shelter they could get. Erin and Emeric started unpacking the gear while Lucky scouted the area. Whenever they camped, Lucky would look around and check their back trail. He would make sure no one was following them or making camp nearby.

Emeric began setting up the canvas structure used to make a shelter to help keep the rain out. By attaching one side of the canvas to the rock wall using anchors fitted into the cracks within the rock; the front side, he held up with adjustable rods, anchoring the front of the canvas to the closest trees.

Erin was busy working on the fire pit. The pit would be right up against the rock wall in the alcove. Allowing the fire to be close to the rock wall would help generate heat off the rock. The smoke would work its way up the rock wall, through the back edge of the canvas shelter, and into the trees on the rim above them, helping to disperse the smoke.

It had been over an hour when Lucky walked into camp. "Nothing to report. Climbed to the top of the rim above us, with great views all around. Did a loop and cut our back trail; not even a gopher insight."

"We need to remember this place next time we're in this area again. This is a great spot to camp and protected from the elements as well," Erin said as she struck the flintstone into the kindling.

"I'll grab the extra packs and see what Yalonda left us." Emeric headed for the packhorse.

Erin and Lucky had the tripod set up, and the cooking pot was already in place over a bristling fire by the time Emeric returned.

"Look at the supplies they gave us." Emeric dug into the pack and started pulling out supplies.

"Dried meats, fruits, nuts; potatoes, jerky, salt, sugar, bacon, several different seasonings, and Pemmican. I think they expected we'd be on the trail for a while. Oh, and look here…flour and yeast. You know what that means?"

"Hotcakes on the fire; Oh, boy!" Lucky replied; it was his favorite.

Emeric, the gun expert, who also enjoyed cooking, put together a wonderful stew and dumplings for the evening meal – and of course, hotcakes would be breakfast in the morning.

The Sun was beginning to wane when they finished cleaning up. Lucky would usually take the first and the last watch beginning at sundown. They split the night watch into two and three-hour segments.

Depending on when they turned in, Lucky would usually take the first couple of hours, Erin would take the next, and Emeric would take the third – he always said that it was easy for him to fall back to sleep after the early morning watch. Lucky would then take the last watch in the morning. He was already a bit high-strung and didn't sleep all that much. If he weren't on the last watch, he still would be up by three or four in the morning.

Morning came early, and Emeric had breakfast made.

"I'll get the horses ready," Lucky said, finishing up his bacon and hotcakes with syrup and honey.

"As good as ever, thanks, Em." Eating was the only time Lucky would thank Emeric for anything – and Emeric had no trouble excepting it.

"You're welcome, any time."

"Great, same time tomorrow?" Lucky replied.

"You got it," Emeric said as he began cleaning up.

"I'll head over and get the horses ready," he repeated. But this time to no one in general.

Lucky got up and headed over to the horses. He felt at ease around the horses. He took good care of them and kept an eye on them while on watch. Erin and Emeric had everything packed up when Lucky brought the horses over. After strapping the packs and gear to the packhorse, they stood by the horses to discuss their day.

Emeric was leaning on his horse with his hand on the saddle horn, "If we continue northeast and just take our time, we could make it there by noon."

"I can secure the town while you and Emeric set up a base camp in one of the old buildings, then you can finish scanning the area while we're there." Lucky was directing his comments to Erin as he climbed onto his horse.

"Good for now, let's hit the trail," Erin replied as she and Emeric climbed onto their horses. They moved out of the trees and into the open.

They rode northeast and reached the Hills of Amidon just before noon. Erin reined in her horse. "Since we're in the hills and haven't been here before, let's take a look around – see if there's anything out of the ordinary before we ride into town."

"I'll ride the south rim," Lucky preferred to ride alone, making it easier to search and explore. "You and Emeric ride the north rim. We can skirt them and do a quick once over in a couple of hours, by the looks of it. Meet you northwest of here in two hours?"

"Works for me," Erin replied. "See you in a few hours."

The company split up and headed into the hills.

Two and a half hours later, all three met up on the hills' far northeastern side. Erin and Emeric were chewing on jerky when Lucky rode up. It was already past noon, and they were hungry. Emeric handed Lucky some jerky when he rode up next to them.

"Thanks," Lucky said. Then he ripped off a large chunk of jerky and proceeded to talk with his mouth full.

"I didn't find anything different. It's all just rocks, trees, and hills. The highest point has some old-line towers lying around. I didn't ride very far in; however, I did ride up a single bluff on the southeast edge." He turned in his saddle and pointed. The others glanced to the south. "Spotted a dust cloud again just a little to the southeast. Could be a large herd slowly heading toward the river."

"They'll often follow the river south, staying close to the water source," Emeric explained.

"How far off you think, Lucky?" Erin asked.

"10 or 12 miles – more or less; get there before sundown."

Erin looked over at Emeric, "Well?"

"We could use the extra meat and fat. It'd keep us well supplied for a while."

"All right then," Erin said as she rode off. And, as usual, the others followed.

They all rode to the top of the hill together. It was two hours before dusk and supper time. When they reached the top, they reined in. Below them, stretching out for what seemed miles, was the largest herd they had ever seen.

"It's bison as far as I can see. How many do you think are here?" Erin asked.

"Could be twenty thousand or more," answered Emeric.

"Were there always this many? I mean before the bombs fell?"

"From what I know, I believe they call this one the Dakota herd. And beyond the Big Horn Mountains, they are called the Big Horn herd. They both are the largest herds in the country. Before the destruction, I heard that the number of bison on this side of the Big Horn Mountains was equal to the herds west of the Big Horns, mostly in the area around Yellowstone. Each area had a herd of about three to four thousand."

"There's just so many of them," Erin expressed.

"There'd be a lot more, but there's a great demand for meat. They say that every 1000 has 300 to 400 calves each season. Take that large number each year and multiply that by the new number of bison able to birth – there could easily be millions of them."

"Every community including Marauders, Ravagers, Scavengers, and people traveling…anyone needing food hunts them," Lucky added.

"Including the Indians!" Emeric pointed to the valley floor below, "to the east along the tree line."

"Do you think it will cause a problem? All we need is one," Erin asked.

"Can't say; let's go find out." Emeric kicked his horse and started down the hill toward the Indians.

"What's he in an all-fired-up hurry for?" Lucky asked with curiosity.

"I think someone has a girlfriend." Erin started down the hill.

"What, wait a minute, what do you mean?" Lucky shouted as Erin made her way down the hill.

He just sat there on his horse, confused by what she meant. "Girlfriend, what girlfriend, why does no one ever tell me these things?" Lucky followed suit with the pack-horse in tow and made his way down the hill.

Chief Two-Kettles received the message of three riders two hours earlier from his scouts. His warriors had spotted the three riders when they crested the hill. He moved out from the tree line to intercept the riders.

Both groups met on the valley floor and rode up face to face.

"Sidanelvhi, welcome extended family," Two-Kettles spoke with joy.

Erin was relieved that it was Two-Kettles and his warriors. She wouldn't exactly know how to approach another band of warriors or hunters.

"Two-kettles, it is such a relief to find you here."

As Erin continued her conversation with Two-kettles, Emeric, who had lagged in the back, slowly turned his horse and headed for the tree line. Neither Lucky nor Erin realized he had left them. Two-Kettles, on the other hand, had watched him go. A slight, discreet grin came over his face. He didn't, however, give it away. His eyes never left Erin as she spoke.

Unbeknown to his partners, Emeric recognized the warriors right away. Realizing Yalonda was not with the Chief, he made his way to the tree line. He believed she was nearby; he could feel her, he could feel her watching him. Making his way into the forest, he was sure she would find him.

"Why are you here? How can we help you?" Two-Kettles asked.

"We saw the herd from a distance and had time to hunt one for some extra meat," Erin replied.

"We will hunt at first light. We will take one extra for you." Chief Two-Kettles declared.

"There's no need. We can shoot our own," Erin replied.

"Very well, Emeric will go with Yalonda; she will show him how we hunt the buffalo."

Both Erin and Lucky suddenly realized that Emeric had not been part of their conversations with Two-Kettles.

Lucky and Erin turned in their saddle and looked around for Emeric.

"He's not here!" Lucky said.

"No, he is gone." Two-Kettles said. "It is alright. He will be back. He will meet us at camp, come now. We have made camp in the woods near a beautiful creek. You will stay with us." Two-Kettles turned his horse, and the warriors moved their horses, allowing him and their guests to pass first before they followed.

Still a little confused about Emeric, they followed Two-Kettles.

Emeric was beginning to feel lost and alone when a familiar voice spoke.

"Emeric!"

When she spoke his name, he felt a chill come over his body. He had no way to explain it. He had never felt anything like it before. Perhaps it was the softness of her voice.

"Emeric, I have found you. Why are you here?" Yalonda moved out from around the darkness of the trees. She knew why he had come into the woods; she wanted to hear it from him.

"We have come to hunt buffalo for meat." Emeric had not caught on. After all, he was new at this.

"No, Emeric. The Sun has moved below the great mountains; the woods are getting dark. Why are you here, in the woods all alone?"

Sitting on his horse, Emeric was afraid, to tell the truth. He didn't know if it was the right thing to do. He was unsure if she felt the same for him as he did for her. Yalonda was patient, and she waited for him to answer.

"I...I came to... into the woods." He stuttered the words, took a moment, then straightened up in his saddle. "I hoped you would find me." He felt more confident and a little relieved.

"Yes, I have found you again. But come. The woods are not a safe place to be alone at night. Come, we will sit by a warm fire…you and I."

Emeric sat there looking down for a few moments: *again? She found me again?* Emeric was lost in his thoughts for a moment, then looked up. She had gotten ahead of him; he put his horse into a trot to catch up.

Lucky and Erin had their camp set up on the edge of the Indian encampment and were sitting near the fire, eating fresh fish from the creek and drinking Indian tea.

"Emeric, there you are. Come over here and try this. The tea comes from an old tribe called the Ojibwe. They call it Swamp Tea, made from maple sugar and honey. Sometimes they add other things to it. They keep it cool, in some jugs, over there in the creek; it tastes better when it's cold. Two-Kettles says it also helps when you get a cold or get sick." Lucky was a little excited.

Emeric reached down and took the wooden cup from Lucky's hand and tasted it. "Nice, it has a smooth sugary taste to it."

"Yea, Two-Kettles says you can boil it down and use it for broth and cooking." Emeric handed the cup back to Lucky.

"I'll see if I can find out how they make it, and we'll give it a try. That is if you can part with some of your beloved syrup?"

"I think I can manage," Lucky replied as he watched Emeric and Yalonda walk away.

Lucky looked over at Erin, who had been watching the scene with interest.

"What's that all about? Is this what you meant earlier?"

They watched as the couple sat down by one of the other three campfires.

It was a restful night for the three of them. No one had to stay awake on watch duty. Emeric was already by the campfire snacking on some bacon and drinking coffee when Lucky and Erin walked up.

"Coffee and bacon smell good," Lucky said. He and Erin sat down and grabbed some bacon.

"Looks like the meat drying racks are ready for after the hunt," Erin said.

Emeric poured a couple of cups of coffee and handed it to them. "I'm told only a handful will stay behind to smoke and jerk some of the meat; easier to carry on the horses. Most of the warriors will leave today. The rest of the meat they will salt and wrap in the bison hides and put them on the wagon." Emeric pointed to the wagon near the horses. "They tell me a hide with salt can preserve the meat for over a week."

"What about our meat?" Erin asked.

"We don't need much, about 25 percent. It takes less than a day to smoke the meat, and they'll smoke it through the night. We'll take the thinner cuts; they should be done sooner. We'll stay tonight. By noon tomorrow, we should be on our way. I'll be riding out with the hunters in a few minutes. Going to learn how they hunt the bison and try and get one for ourselves."

"Yalonda going to help you with that?" Lucky asked with a smug grin on his face.

Emeric knew what Lucky was doing. "As a matter of fact, she is," Emeric said with a bit of pride in his voice.

"Good," Erin replied. She sipped her coffee. "We're going to the top of the hill just south of here. Two-Kettle's scouts said the herd didn't move during the night but are starting to now."

Emeric stood up. "The hunters have found a place to strike from, so I'll see you when it's over." He turned and headed for the horses.

Lucky and Erin stood with the Chief and a few braves at the top of the hill. They could see a reasonable distance to the north and the south. South of them, the bison herd slowly moved. The north end of the herd had not yet begun to move. In the distance, they could see a dividing fork on the valley floor.

They watched as hunters made their way to the rocks and boulders around the division at the fork. The plan was to startle the northern part of the herd, pushing them south. As they stampeded, they'd split at the fork.

On foot, Emeric followed Yalonda to a rocky outcropping of boulders. There were six hunters, counting Yalonda and Emeric. The goal was to take down 20 bison. Twenty would feed the tribe for months. Hunting and trapping through the winter will offset their food supply.

"Two hunters will move near the rear of the herd. Together they will shoot at a buffalo, maybe take two down right away," Yalonda began to explain. "The bison are already moving south. The sound of their rifles will startle them; they will run our way. The riders will follow from behind, keeping them moving. The buffalo will be close to us, some on the right, some on the left. We must watch over the boulder and shoot from there. The hunters will try to take four each. Take one or two if you like, but don't shoot any until you see the end of the herd. If we shoot too soon, the bison will trample the dead on the ground, and the meat will go to waste."

"Good point," Emeric replied.

Five minutes later, two rifle shots rang out. Within two minutes, they could hear the hoofs' pounding getting louder and louder; the ground began to shake. They climbed on top of the large boulder, took their aim, and waited. They could see the rear of the herd running, but the section near them was walking. Suddenly the herd began to bunch up. The front was not moving as fast as the rear.

Soon they started splitting at the fork. Bison were running both on the left and the right of them now. The dust was getting heavier, the sound of the hoofs almost deafening. Fear swept over Emeric; he kept it in check. It wasn't easy to breathe. He couldn't' see the end of the herd. It was a terrifying and exciting site. Bison weighing up to 2000 lbs. moved past them at a terrific speed.

"It's time,' Yalonda shouted.

Rifles fired from both sides of them. Yalonda fired, and a buffalo came to a sliding stop right up to the front of the boulder.

"Best to shoot when they are coming right at you, easier to hit in the front, between the legs," Yalonda shouted.

The sounds of the rifles mixed with the sound of the hoofs pounding the earth – Emeric was so enthralled with the hunt - watching these magnificent creatures, he almost forgot about the shooting.

Emeric steadied his rifle and watched for one to come at him. When he had one in sight, he squeezed the trigger just before the animal turned. It lost its footing, rolled, and came to a stop away from the stampede. The other hunters had stopped shooting. Emeric set his sight on a bison near the end of the herd; he fired, and the animal dropped just as the last of them passed by.

Emeric took an unexpected deep breath. He held his breath longer than expected while waiting to take the buffalo down. When he climbed down off of the boulder, he still felt out of breath and took a moment to breathe.

"That was a little more excitement than I've had in a long time," Emeric said to Yalonda.

"You did good. You got two. Emeric the Hunter." She was proud of him.

"That was so amazing I almost forgot to shoot."

Altogether, the hunting party took 21 bison. Yalonda and Emeric got five. Two hunters got three each, and two got four each; the riders pushing the herd took down two.

When Emeric and Yalonda walked out to the open prairie, the hunters and warriors were already skinning the bison. Emeric had once heard that early hunters could shoot 200 bison in a day and skin one in five minutes hundreds of years ago. The Indians weren't far off. Already they were making good work of it and beginning to cut meat. Emeric and Yalonda jumped in and started helping.

Everything the Indians required from the bison had been taken within a few hours. Strips of beef were already hanging on the smoke racks. Thin slices were laid out on rocks in the Sun to dry. The hide-wrapped meat and other hides and parts of the animal were being packed into the wagon, as much as it could carry.

It was past noon, and the warriors had everything packed. The wagon and riders began to move out. Two-Kettles had said his goodbyes earlier. They could lose no time getting the supplies back to the village.

Yalonda was tying down the packs on her saddle when Emeric walked up behind her. He touched her shoulder and turned her around.

"I wish you didn't have to leave," he said to her.

"I have work to finish back home; I must go. Again, we must go our own way. I am going to miss you – Emeric the Hunter."

"And I will miss you."

Yalonda put her hands on his face. Emeric's knees went weak. She spoke to him softly.

"Twice, I have found you. The first, the day we met, I found you; and then, yesterday in the woods, I found you again. Next time you will find me. I have seen this."

"I do? I will!" Emeric stuttered.

Yalonda leaned in and kissed him on the lips. Emeric froze from the unanticipated surprise.

"See you soon, my Emeric the Hunter." Yalonda climbed onto her horse, smiled at him, turned, and rode for home.

CHAPTER 7

They turned northwest and met up with an old gravel road overgrown from years of weeds, wild grasses and wheat that had blown in from nearby fields. The team followed it north to the old paved highway. The red and white stop sign was still standing. All three stopped and looked in both directions as if a car or truck might pass by.

There were no cars, trucks, or no fuel to operate them. None of them had even driven a vehicle; they only sat in those abandoned and scattered along old roadways. Yet, the instinct to look both ways was in their blood, still woven into the DNA from generations long passed. All three pulled out onto the highway without considering their unusual behavior and made a left-hand turn.

They stopped less than a mile from town to observe. Erin noticed something green on the side of the road. She got down from her horse, walked into the ditch, and started pulling weeds and dry grass away from it.

"It's an old road sign." She lifted it for the others to see. "It says, 'White Butte' at the top."

"Ya, looks like butt," Lucky said.

"No, it's butte. Butt doesn't have an 'e' after the 't.'"

"The rest of it says, 'highest point in North Dakota, Elevation 3506 ft.'."

"So, if the sign is on this side of the road, the arrow would point toward the hills. You don't suppose the highest point of the Hills of Amidon was named White Butte?" asked Emeric.

"Well, I would say your observation might be correct."

Erin looked at the sign for a few more moments before she let it drop back onto the ground.

As she climbed back into the saddle, she asked. "What do you think, Lucky? Does the town look clear?"

"Looks calm… I didn't see any fresh horses dropping on our way here. Been watching for signs of movement ever since we could see the town from the hills and nothing," Lucky stated.

"Why don't you take the long way around; Em and I will ride straight in."

"Got it," he replied.

Lucky turned his horse north. He was going to make a wide loop around the north side of town, make his way, as quietly as he could, onto a roof of one of the buildings, rifle in tow, to monitor Emeric and Erin as they made their way into town. Spotting a small barn structure, he rode over. The rooftop was high enough to see the surrounding area and close enough to the ground for him to climb onto.

Lucky pulled his horse up next to the building, pulled his rifle from the sheath, and ground reined his horse. Standing on the saddle, he reached up, laid his rifle on the roof, and climbed up. He made it to the top just in time to see Emeric and Erin come into town.

Erin and Emeric walked their horse right down main, guns ready, hoping to draw anyone out rather than spending the time to search for them. No signs of anyone and no sounds from Lucky.

"Either the town is clear, or they're hiding from us," Emeric said to Erin.

"The only people who might hide would be Wanderers. They don't normally camp in a town, and I'm pretty sure there aren't any around here this time of year."

"I didn't think anyone would be as stupid to be here as we are," Emeric replied.

"Don't look at me," proclaimed Erin. "You let Lucky talk us into coming back here."

Erin reined to a stop. Emeric passed her, turned his horse around, and walked it a couple of steps back. Erin was looking over at a building.

"What is it?" Emeric said.

"This is the bar that we scavenged."

"Ya! So!"

"The door is open!"

Erin rode over, got down off her horse, handed the reins to Emeric, and walked to the door. The door was about half open. She grabbed the door handle and pulled it closed. Erin walked over to where Emeric was tying the horses to an old pole once used as an overhang on the building's front.

"So, what's the problem?"

"When we left, I know I pulled the door closed."

"They're old buildings. The wind probably pushed it open."

"No, I remember. The door was still shut tight. The wind couldn't have pushed it open."

Emeric walked over and gave the door a hard push. "You're right; it's solid. Smells like fish to me."

"Fish? How can you smell fish?"

"It smells like fish, like something is wrong."

"Stop saying that; you're making me hungry. And the expression is that *something smells fishy*. I'm going to have a look inside."

"Not without me." Emeric grabbed his rifle off the horse and followed her in as he mumbled something about Fish and Chips.

When inside, they both stopped and looked around.

"Doesn't look any different to me," Emeric said.

"Does to me, I can feel it. The chairs are out of place; the tables are not as dusty. There should be scuff marks and handprints all over it from when we sat here before; it seems to have been dusted off."

Erin headed for the office, where she found the whiskey bottle. When inside, she headed straight for the file cabinet.

"Someone's been here, alright. When I pulled up the floorboard, I put it into the file drawer just in case nails were sticking out of it. I didn't want to step on it. Now it's laying over by the wall as if someone picked it up, then just tossed it."

Erin got down on her knees and looked into the hole she had pulled the ammo box. "Looks like someone was digging around in here; hard to tell, though." On her knees, Erin turned her head and looked toward the door. She quickly got up and went to the door, peeked around it, and into the main bar area. "it's gone!"

"What's gone?" Emeric said.

"The ammo box - we left it on top of the bar. It's gone."

Both walked out of the office and stood beside the bar where they had left the ammo box.

"Rats!" Emeric said with a saddened look on his face. "I liked that ammo box."

"No sense crying over spilled milk."

"What milk? Emeric quizzed.

"Never mind." Erin headed for the door; Emeric followed behind like a curious little boy.

"Wait, what milk are you talking about?"

"Drop it; it's nothing."

Erin, herself, didn't understand the phrase either. It was just something her mother used to say when she wanted something she couldn't have or when something broke.

When Erin and Emeric got outside, Lucky was sitting on his horse; leaning down on his saddle horn.

"You two kids having fun in there?"

"No!" Emeric replied. "Erin won't tell me what she meant by 'spilled milk.'"

"Milk?" Lucky piped up. "You guys got milk?"

"No! There's no milk, no one's drinking milk, and no one spilled any milk… it was just a stupid expression. Now, would you two drop it? We need to find a place to set up a base camp.

Both Emeric and Lucky had a disappointed look on their face. Lucky leaned over to Emeric and whispered.

"It's a monthly thing, isn't it?"

"I heard that," Erin snorted.

"When we were here last, I hid out in the old courthouse. You can tell the tower structure was added sometime later; it doesn't match the main building. It's very thick; a bomb couldn't blast through. It has three floors, including the roof with circular stairways around the tower wall. The third floor has narrow windows added with a latch on top. It's like a gun turret. You can see all around town from there. If I didn't know any better, I'd say it was a lookout tower, used as a defensive position."

"Sounds like a good place to set up basecamp. We could use a defensive position if anyone is looking to make trouble," Emeric said.

"Let's do it. I'm getting hungry, and you two are getting on my nerves." Erin knew it was all in fun, and she would laugh at it later. But right now, she was tired and hungry. Tomorrow she'd feel better.

Behind the old courthouse was an attached garage area to shelter the horses. The garage doors were still attached, which would help keep the horses out of view. Lucky would have the horses out grazing by the end of his watch in the morning. They entered onto the main floor of the watchtower through the garage. The room had no windows. The door to their right entered the main building. The third opened to the back of the building. All the doors were extra heavy steel-framed, still intact and convenient.

All three quickly explored the building; basecamp was set up on the original building's main floor, the rooms nearest the watchtower door. These rooms at the rear of the building were probably offices, used for overnight rooms more recently. Erin chose a separate room for herself. It had been a long time since she could sleep without listening to snoring. The room Lucky and Emeric would share had metal bunk beds built into the wall; the mattresses were long gone.

The kitchen and break room were located near the center of the building. The main floor had bars over the outside of the windows, making it difficult to enter through; something added on later for security. The watchtower's upper floors and three exits gave them a tactical advantage.

Emeric looked over at Erin, "if you two get camp set up, I'll get the kitchen cleaned up and start making dinner."

Everyone agreed, and they all went to work. When Emeric got to the kitchen, he examined every cabinet and drawer. There was nothing of use. The good news; the stovetop oven area was converted into a firepit, of sorts, with a grill that fits on top of the stove.

The top and guts inside the oven had all been removed. The fan above the stove was removed; exposing the vent allowed the heat and smoke to vent directly out of the building. Someone had done an excellent job designing the oven/firepit.

Emeric went outside through the watchtower's back door and gathered wood from around the old fallen trees. Lucky and Erin were busy unpacking the horses. Lucky put all the food supplies in the kitchen for Emeric.

When Emeric returned, he put the wood down inside the oven and started the fire—opening the oven door allowing easy access to the fire. Air vents were cut into the stove just above and below the firepit, making the firepit practically smokeless. Any remaining smoke flowed nicely up and through the vent flue. Emeric put the grill top on the stove and got busy cleaning up.

Emeric could hear Erin and Lucky through the open doors. "They packed us some bison hump in a hide; we can have bison steaks for a week or more.," he said. "I think I'll simmer up some bison stew tomorrow with dumplings. Tonight, I'm making some Bannock bread and steak slices."

Both Erin and Lucky had stopped what they were doing and were now standing in the doorway. Emeric continued to talk loud as if they were still in the other room.

"Got a special treat tonight as well. Got some fruit preserves and some of that Swamp tea Lucky likes."

"How'd you get that," Lucky asked while standing behind Emeric.

"Lucky, I swear, I'm going to water the weeds with that tea if you don't stop sneaking up on me!"

"I'm sorry, I forgot. I promise I won't do it again."

Erin noticed Lucky had his fingers crossed behind his back.

"Don't trust him, Em," Erin said, leaning against the door jam. "Might as well dump that Swamp Water now." With a smile on her face, she turned and left the room.

"NO, NO, NO! Please, I won't do it again," Lucky pleaded.

"Very well, help yourself. It's on the counter behind you. It's not cold, but it might be nice to heat up this evening for tea."

Lucky poured a small amount into a mug just to try it. "Yep, tastes much better cold. I mean, it's alright; it might be better heated up." Emeric shook his head in agreement, and Lucky went back to work, setting up their camp in the other room.

Before dinner, Lucky found some mixed-matched chairs and a table in the building. Erin helped him set them up in the kitchen. The campfire stove kept the room warm. Evenings were cooling down. The conversation centered around the bison hunt. Emeric was reliving his adventures but didn't realize he talked more about Yalonda than the hunt. Erin and Lucky just sat and listened with a smile on their faces.

Lucky caught a break to jump in when Emeric took a breath. "So how did you manage to get all these extra supplies?

"Well, it might be a matter of who you know," Emeric said.

Erin spoke up. "And who do you know?" She and Lucky already knew the answer. But it was not what they were expecting.

"The chief's daughter," Emeric said with a big grin.

Erin and Lucky just looked at each other. At about the same time, they both said, "you don't mean…."

Emeric broke in, "Yalonda."

"What, no way," Lucky said with the sound of shock in his voice.

Erin just smiled as Emeric answered Lucky's curious questions. She was happy for him and had never seen him like this. She wasn't jealous, maybe a little envious, wishing she could feel the way Emeric felt.

Erin was able to chime in when the boy's conversation calmed down. "I'd like to scavenge this building tomorrow since we're already here. Lucky, can you manage the horses in the morning and throughout the day and keep watch; It might be a good opportunity to look over this watchtower. You don't just build such a nice watchtower without…you know; more to it."

"Sounds like a good idea," Lucky replied.

"I'll take first watch tonight; give me a chance to check out the watchtower myself," Erin said.

After dinner cleanup, they hit the sack; it was a workday tomorrow.

It was early morning, and Lucky had already tended the horses. Emeric had bacon and flapjacks ready to go.

"Where do you think you want to start?" Emeric asked as Erin ate her bacon and jack.

"Thought about taking a better look around this building…get a better feel for it."

Erin did a thorough walkthrough of the building. Hard to tell if it had been scavenged before or just destroyed for the fun of it. Drywall and broken furniture were scattered throughout the room.

Scavengers wouldn't do this kind of damage. Erin went into the room she was staying in and grabbed the carry case. One by one, she scanned the rooms on a low setting so the Light Bender wouldn't scan all the way through the walls. The fourth room was the nicest of all the office rooms. It was apparent this was the office of a person in charge. Although it had once been charming, the furniture and desk were now beyond use.

Erin opened the three legs to the tripod and locked her Light Bender onto it. The tripod mount had a connecting stem that stood straight up from the center. Erin would place the round orb onto the tripod with a small hole in the center. It locked in automatically. When she was finished and ready to remove it, she'd put both hands on it, and it would automatically detach. She could then lift it off.

It was noon, and Erin was beginning to get hungry. She had been at it for five hours, and the smell of Emeric's cooking made her stomach growl.

Leaning outside the door and into the hallway, Erin softly hollered, "Emeric, how long before lunch?"

"It's ready now if you like. Lucky's already had his." The voice came back from the kitchen.

Erin left her equipment where it was and walked over to the kitchen. Emeric had mixed the beans with the extra bacon from the morning breakfast. Seasonings were peppered onto the fresh Bannock bread from the stove.

"Did you know this bread was first made hundreds of years ago by the Scots who cooked it over a fire on a griddle called a Bannock stone?"

"Where did you learn that?" Erin asked.

"From an old mountain man I met living and trapping in the Big Horns. He's the one who taught me how to cook on the fire. He said the Indians used to live in a place called

Reservations. The Indians there would make fry bread, similar to this bread but flatter, and put toppings of finely ground beef with beans and seasoning. They called it Indian Tacos."

"Well, I don't know how that would have tasted, but this is sure darn good."

"Thanks," Emeric replied.

After Erin helped Emeric do some cleaning up, she headed back to the office to finish her scans. She touched the Light Bender to activate it, took the handheld control module out of the bag, and pushed the power button. Adjusting the module for a low-density scan, Erin set the five-minute timer. Then picked up the case and, with the control module, walked out of the room.

After the timer sounded, Erin returned to the office and set the control module on the desk. She took the Light Bender off the stand and put it back into its carry case. Picking up the module, she adjusted the setting to PMS, Panoramic Material Scan, and started her search. Slowly pointing the module around the room, she didn't see anything within the walls.

She pointed the screen of the control module to the ceiling and moved it around; nothing. She did the same with the floor. The only thing she picked up was a safe in the floor behind the desk. Erin laid the control module on the desk then pulled her flashlight out of the carry case.

On the floor where she located a safe, an old beat-up rug lay over it. She carefully moved it away so as not to kick up any dust. The floor safe had the typical covering over it. A couple of floorboards were made into a trap door with a thin inset handle and hinges. Erin lifted the trap door revealing the safe. If locked, it would take some time to open it, which was a job for Lucky. However, it was always best to try the handle first if unlocked. And it was.

Erin lifted the heavy safe door open and shined her flashlight inside, but the safe was empty. She suspected as much. If whoever was here were bugging out, they would have taken anything of value in the safe, usually leaving it unlocked. They would then have closed it back up and put the carpet back over so no one would trip over it as they were preparing to leave.

Earlier, Erin passed by a door leading into a small closet-size room with metal file cabinets. She decided to scan this room next. On both sides of the wall, cabinets were lined. Nothing else showed up on the scanner, so she started going through them one drawer at a time fingering through the files.

Putting her hand inside, she felt around for anything unusual. The file cabinets contained property, county, and other miscellaneous documents. There were books on local laws, state laws, and other legal books. But one book stood out, different than the rest. It was a hand-printed book in a self-made leather binding. On the front, it read *The Healers Guide To Nanomedicine.* Erin walked out of the room, paging through the book and checking out the front and back cover. "Might make a nice addition to my library. I'll have to read some of it later," she said aloud.

Erin did quick work at scanning the rest of the old building. Next, she headed for the garage. Tomorrow, she would explore the watchtower. She was tired of scanning, and the garage would be the last of the day. Besides,

Emeric had already begun simmering the bison stew, and the smell was making her hungry.

She set up the Light Bender on the tripod stand, activated it, set the control on the module to a higher setting, then set the timer to 10 minutes so the orb would scan slower and deeper into the cement area around the garage. After the timer sounded, she put away her Light Bender and then pointed the module screen around the garage. There was nothing in the garage - until she pointed the module toward the watchtower door.

The walls looked to be three to five feet deep. She glanced at the text in a column on the right side of the screen. It gave metal content and other information. She read cement and metal. She thought it looked like ordinary cement. However, it did look like an open space in the thickest part of the tower wall.

Erin walked over and put her hands on the cement wall. She turned around, looking at the Light Bender, then the surrounding garage area. *Maybe it's emitting a reflection off of the cement from the watchtower to the open space in the garage.* She turned and stared at the wall for a while longer, deep in thought, before packing everything up for the day.

CHAPTER 8

It was tough for them to roll out of bed this morning. Maybe it was the bison stew and Bannock bread everyone ate too much of, or perhaps Lucky's hot Swamp Tea put them into a somniferous tea hangover.

Even Lucky, who's usually up moving around, and acting like it's the middle of the day, came dragging into the kitchen. Emeric was cooking over the campfire stove.

"I am not drinking anymore of that tea of yours," glancing at Lucky. It was the first words out of Emeric since he woke up.

Lucky plopped himself down in a chair at the table and put his head down. "I dragged all night, couldn't keep awake. You think it was the tea?"

"Whatever it was, help put us to sleep." Emeric slurred.

"Where's Erin?"

"When I walked out of our room this morning, I could hear her snoring."

"I heard that," Erin said as she slumbered through the kitchen door. "Breakfast does smell good. I hope the coffee will wake me up."

"It'll help."

Emeric poured coffee from the pot heated by the fire into her mug and set it on the table. He paused and looked at Lucky. His head was still on the table. Emeric reached over and poured a cup for Lucky and set it next to him.

"Drink the coffee. You're gonna need it."

Lucky slowly lifted his head and looked at the cup, "thanks," was all he could spit out.

It took most of the morning for them to wake up. Emeric cleaned around the kitchen; Lucky and Erin went on a short walk around town. It was a beautiful fall day.

The trees in town were changing color. The grass that needed cutting was green and soft. They could imagine the lovely, well-kept homes with people walking by and visiting each other. It was quiet and peaceful. A light breeze swept through the trees swirling the leaves around them. How peaceful, how friendly it must have been before the ravage of the wars.

Erin and Lucky met Emeric in the kitchen, sitting at the table drinking coffee; he had made a second pot.

"More coffee?" Erin asked.

Emeric nodded toward the pot.

Erin looked at Lucky, "want another?"

"Ya, thanks." Lucky sat down in a chair.

Erin walked back to the table with two mugs, sat down, and slid one over to Lucky.

"When I was scanning the garage yesterday, I pointed the module toward the wall where the door is. It looked a little strange. I don't know if it was just a reflection coming off the cement from the watchtower; it looked like there was a space in the tower wall."

"How large a space?" Emeric asked.

"The cement walls looked five feet thick, so maybe...four feet."

"If you scan the main level of the watchtower, you think you can tell for sure?"

"I'm pretty sure - if I get the settings right."

"Can I help?" Lucky pipped up. "I don't often get to be around when you find things. That'd be fun to see."

Erin looked over at Emeric.

"I do need to get out and get some fresh air. I can go for a walk, have a look around and keep watch. Maybe I'll climb to the watchtower roof, take a chair, watch, and just hang out in the nice weather."

"Looks like you're with me today Lucky."

"Great, let's get started."

"Okay, let's go," Erin sighed and dragged herself out of the chair.

She headed to her room to gather up her equipment. Lucky followed.

"Take the tripod and the Findings Bag for me." Erin picked up the carry case and headed to the watchtower. Lucky followed with eagerness.

When Erin and Lucky walked onto the watchtower's main level, Erin sat her case down and stood there looking around. Lucky followed suit.

The watchtower room was more of a seating area or waiting area for someone to do business at the courthouse. Along the wall on the northside of the watchtower, the same side the door entered into the courthouse; there were chairs and benches; most of them broken.

On the east and west side of the tower, the doors opened to the garage and the back of the courthouse. On the south wall were built-in bookshelves. Perhaps used for books and magazines; something for people to look at while they waited.

"Set up the tripod here in the center." Erin pointed to a spot on the floor for Lucky.

Kneeling, Erin opened the carry case that held the orb-shaped scanner; her Light Bender activated when she picked it up. When Lucky finished, Erin put the scanner onto the tripod's stem. It locked into place. "When I finished early yesterday, I didn't get all the devices charged. I hope there's enough power to last."

Erin picked up the control module and pushed the power button to turn on the module and computer screen. As the unit powered up, a single beep was heard from somewhere other than the module; they looked at each other.

"Where'd that come from?" Erin asked.

Lucky shrugged his shoulders, "not sure; it sounded like it came from the bookshelves.

Erin laid her module back into the open case, and they both walked over to the bookshelves. The shelves were only an inch thick but had a two-inch false front making the shelf boards look thicker.

"Lucky, go to the far end of the bookcase and start feeling around everything. Let me know if you feel anything unusual. We'll work our way to the center.

Lucky started on the far end, methodically searching every inch of the bookcase with his fingers, but found nothing. Halfway through the following case, he felt something unusual on the underside of the shelf.

"Found something." Lucky got down on his knees as Erin walked over to him.

Lucky stuck his head into the bookcase and looked at the underside of the shelf, "wow, look at this!"

He got out and moved over, still on his knees.

Erin got down and looked under the shelf. "It looks like a scanner screen.

It's only about two inches square." Erin paused for a few moments thinking.

"Oh…I don't believe it."

"What?" Lucky asked.

"It's a finger scanner, a touchpad. I've only seen pictures and read about them in one of my books."

"A finger scanner…for what?"

"To scan the fingerprint. Every person's fingerprint is different. None are the same. When you place your finger on the screen, it scans your print and tells the computer who you are."

"What's the purpose of that?" Lucky was getting curious.

"The purpose," Erin repeated, "is to tell the computer you have clearance to go through a door."

"Why would they put that here. The only doors here are the ones we use."

"Think about it? The scanner is hidden so nobody can see it."

On their knees, Erin waited.

Lucky began to reach into his pocket.

"Don't do it!"

"Don't do what?"

"Don't pull that knife out of your pocket and pick your teeth with it. Think without it."

"Fine," Lucky huffed, then stood up. Erin stood up and walked over to the carry case.

"So, If I walked into this room," Lucky looked over at the door to the garage.

"Coming through that door, I walk over here, and without having to bend over or reach up…I just place my finger under the shelf and touch the pad." Lucky walked through the scenario, including putting his finger on the touchpad.

"So, if I touch it standing here, where is the door?"

"Let's find out." Erin picked up the control module. The unit was still powered up.

"Lucky, take a look at this!"

He walked over and looked at the computer screen with Erin.

"When I powered up the module, it must have activated the touchpad. There are two new buttons on the screen I've never seen before."

"What's that say?" Lucky pointed at the screen.

"I know you don't read well, but I think you can read these words."

Lucky started to read them slowly. "In…it..."

"Initiate." Erin helped.

"Thanks. Initiate Door Lock. Is that right?"

"It is; try the next."

"De..act…tiv.. Deactivate Door Lock."

"You did good. Sorry I haven't helped with your reading. We'll have to start working on it again."

"Sure, no problem. So, what does it mean?"

"To Initiate means to start or begin. In this case, I believe it would be to turn on the door lock. You initiate the lock when you shut the door, thereby locking the door. When you deactivate it…"

"You open the lock," he interrupted.

"Right. Then the door should open. I don't understand why, but the control module has activated this touch-pad for some unknown reason. Should we try it? You get the honors. You found the touchpad – touch the button on the screen."

Lucky reached over and touched the button.

Suddenly a whining sound came from the bookcase, then a puff of air and dust came out from around the sides of the same shelves. Lucky's jaw dropped as the bookcase slid back into the wall allowing enough room to walk through.

"A secret door, I don't believe it. How awesome is that?" Lucky was elated.

"It's awesome; however, I need you to go find Emeric. We're not doing any exploring unless he's with us."

Lucky bolted out the back door of the watchtower. Erin went back to her room, put on her sidearm, and grabbed her sling pack. She was already in the tower when Lucky and Emeric came through the back door.

"Well, would you look at that?" Emeric stood there looking at the hidden door, his hands on his hips. "What you wanna do?"

Erin took the flashlight out of the carry case. "Do you think it's safe enough outside for all of us to go?"

"The towns quiet. Should be Okay," Emeric replied.

"Good. Since you two already have your guns, I'll let you take the light and clear the room." She handed the flashlight to Emeric.

"I'll take the Light Bender in with me next. I can turn on the scanner lights; they're bright enough to light up about a six-to-eight-foot area around us."

"I'm going to carry the Light Bender. Lucky, I need you to carry the control module."

Erin scrolled down the screen on the module to Live Scan and touched it; the scanner activated. She then scrolled to the setting that read *Illum*—referring to Illuminate. She handed the module to Lucky, walked over to the tripod, and removed the Orb.

"When we get inside, touch the Illum button. Keep an eye on the screen. It will show you everything around us. If you see something unusual, let me know. I have it on Live Scan. However, if the sensors inside it sense anything dangerous, it will sound off. Got it?"

"Got it," Lucky answered.

Emeric was looking through the opening when Erin and Lucky walked up behind him. Emeric looked back at them.

"It's not a room. It's a staircase going down." Emeric moved over so Erin could look around him. Emeric held the flashlight with the beam facing down the stairs.

"There's an Open/Close button on the wall," she said.

"Yea, but I think we should prop the door open just to be on the safe side. Lucky, grab me one of those broken chair legs over there."

Lucky brought one over and handed it to Emeric. Forcing the leg between the bottom edge of the door and the bookcase door, Emeric said, "That should do it."

"Alright, after you," Erin said a little fearfully.

Emeric started down the staircase, his handgun in one hand and the flashlight in the other. Erin followed, holding her Light Bender in front of her. When Lucky came through the opening, he touched the button; the scanner lit up the staircase with a bright bluish glow.

Ten feet down, they came to the bottom of the staircase. It was just a small platform. Around the corner, the stairs continued downward. When they reached the next section, it was the same, continuing down. They'd gone down five flights when they finally got to the bottom.

"I am not looking forward to climbing that later," Lucky said when he reached the bottom. Emeric and Erin were standing in front of another door.

"Lucky, come over here and put the module in front of this entry keypad."

The entry lock on this door was different. It had a finger touchpad and a 10-key push-button pad. Lucky walked over and pointed the module at the scanner.

"It's the same but with four numbers above lock buttons; two, four, six, and eight," said Lucky.

Erin looked over at the screen. "It must be giving us a passcode to use. Touch each number, then touch the Deactivate Lock button; see if that works.

Lucky slowly began touching the passcode numbers saying each number aloud, "two, four, six, eight; how do we deactivate." Lucky looked up with a smile of satisfaction on his face.

Both Erin and Emeric were looking at him.

"Don't ever do that again," Emeric said firmly.

Erin turned away with a grin on her face.

Just then, the door squeaked and whined. Air was released after years of being sealed tight; the door slowly swung open.

Emeric stepped into the doorway and pointed his flashlight down a long hallway.

"What ya think all the doors are?" Lucky asked, peeking around Emeric.

"Only one way to find out." Emeric walked into the hallway.

When he got to the first door, he stopped and looked at the name on the door. Erin walked up next to him. The name on the door read *Dr. R. Galloway*.

"The D-R stands for Doctor. The other R. is the letter for the first name, and the last name is Galloway," Erin said.

Emeric turned the doorknob, slowly opened the door, then peeked in with his flashlight.

"It's a small living quarter with a bed," Emeric said with curiosity in his voice.

Erin pushed the door open and walked in using the light radiating from the orb. She walked around the room; a bed was still neatly made with a pillow. Next to it was a small dresser with a lamp. Erin opened each drawer. Nothing but dust bunnies. Beyond that, a small stainless-steel sink with a counter, a mirror, and light above it. The only thing sitting on the sink was a toothbrush holder.

Moving along the next wall was a long metal closet. Lucky pulled the doors open. It had dresser drawers inside and a hanging bar. A couple of shirts were still hanging in the closet, and a white jacket and extra hangers. Lucky pulled out one of the shirts. It was a Navy-blue dress shirt; the other was white. They were in excellent condition from being sealed underground.

"Nice shirt, should fit me too."

Erin pulled open the top drawer of the dresser. "And look, a couple of matching ties to go with it." Lucky leaned over to look. The other drawers were empty.

Next to the closet was a metal desk in the corner. It had a desk light and a chair with wheels. Erin went through the drawers. Nothing they needed, just desk supplies, pens, pencils, paperclips, stapler, etc.

When Erin finished, she and Lucky walked back out into the hallway. Emeric was standing on the edge of the doorway, keeping watch.

"Looks like about twelve doors or rooms down this hallway. The last few seem to have a window."

"We'll open each door, clear the rooms, and then we can go through them sometime later," Erin voiced.

One by one, they opened each door and looked inside, leaving the doors open. They cleared eight living quarters. The tenth door on the right was called the *Maintenance Control Center/Shelter*. Emeric turned the door handle and slowly pushed the heavy door open. "Look at this. It's a thick steel framed door." Emeric walked around, examining the door and the door jamb; he continued. "On the outside, it opens like a regular door. But it has bolts in the door that lock into the door jam. Emeric began turning the large wheel handle on the backside of the door. The bolts slowly moved out. He then turned the bolts back in.

Erin took a moment to look around. "It's a sheltered control center."

She took her time walking around and reading all the tags on the equipment; *HVAC System, Fresh Air Exchange/Filtration.*

"That's interesting," she said out loud. The air exchange system has a switch you can change from Fresh Air to Recirculate Air."

She continued to walk around*: Backup Generator, Well Pump, Collection and Water Filtration, and Waste Management.* Most of the conduits were marked: *Plumbing and electricity*.

A large metal unit built into the cement wall was on the far wall with panel lights and a computer screen and keyboard. Next to it was a built-in desk with six small computer screens and a control board. Erin glanced around the desk to a metal door with the same large wheel handle as the door they came in. She didn't think much of it. Her mind hadn't yet taken in everything.

Erin walked past Lucky and Emeric back into the hallway, "Everything needed for self-containment," she said. "Let's move on."

Emeric moved to the next room across the hall and began to open the door.

"Probably the Restroom," Erin said as Emeric opened the door.

After opening the door and looking inside, Emeric turned back with a grin. "Thanks a lot, you're hilarious…you read the sign on the door."

"Sorry," Erin teased, "I couldn't resist."

"Look at this." Lucky was looking through the glass window next to them. "It's a kitchen."

Emeric shined his light through the window, "nice," he stated, then opened the door and went inside. The others followed.

"Wow, this is nice and big. Look at all the storage space," Emeric quickly walked over to a large unit with two doors, "Oh ya, they called this a commercial cooler or unit, a refrigerator to keep your food cold."

Erin walked over and opened a door next to the cooler. Glancing inside the room was the width of the kitchen. Along the wall were shelves stacked with supplies. Emeric glanced inside with his flashlight.

"I definitely will be going through this later."

Everyone walked back over into the kitchen area. Emeric reached out and grabbed the handle of the commercial cooler.

"Stop!" Erin shouted, "don't open that door!"

Emeric looked over at her, "why?'

"Can you imagine the smell from all the rotten food inside?"

Emeric looked at the door with an unusual look on his face. He put his ear on the door. Then he went around to the unit's side and put his hand on it near the rear. "It running."

"What?" Erin said.

"It's warm," Emeric put his ear on the unit again. "The motor is running. I can hear it."

"How's that possible?" Lucky asked.

"I don't know." Emeric went back to the front and opened the door."

Erin quickly put both hands up as to say, No Stop; but said nothing.

Lucky walked over and looked inside the lighted refrigerator unit. "You think any of that stuff… is still any good? How old do you suppose it is? Twenty to 40 years?"

"Some of it might be. The question is…why?"

"My thoughts exactly," Erin stated. Now that I think about it. How did the two entry scanners have power? Did we even try any of the light switches?"

Lucky walked over to the door and flipped the switch next to it. The lights flickered then on.

They all stood there looking up at the lights. Erin swung her sling pack around, unzipped it, and put the Light Bender into it. She went out the door and across the hall and into the Control Center; the others followed. Once inside, Erin reached over and turned on the lights. Some of the control lights on the large unit at the room's rear flickered as she did. She then walked over to the computer and touched one of the keys on the computer keyboard. The screen opened to a maintenance power grid. The readings indicated that power usage was minimal.

Referring to the control panel, Erin explained. "The reason the refrigerator unit was still running, and the entry units still had power; they require very little power to operate when not in use. So, it's like everything is sleeping. When you opened the door to the unit, it kicked in a little more power. More or less waking everything up. When I came into the room and turned the lights on, the colored lights on this panel lit up, kicking in more power."

"So, where's it getting power from?" Emeric asked.

"From itself."

Emeric and Lucky just looked at each other. "You mean, like the Light Bender?" Emeric suspected.

"Yes, exactly," She answered. "When I read the computer screen, the program that it's operating under is called NEMO Systems. It stands for *Nuclear Electromagnetic Molecular Operating Systems;* in short, it's Nano energy. Like the Light Bender, it's a self-contained nuclear power source that will last…well, pretty much forever."

"Are you saying that we could live here forever and always have power…I could keep my Swamp Tea cold!" Lucky said somewhat excitedly.

They ignored him.

Erin sat down at the computer keyboard and did a little exploring.

"I can set the system's electrical settings to its IR or Inferred settings. So, when we walk by, any of the switches or other IR systems should power up, and the lights should turn on."

When they walked back out into the hall, all the lights down the hallway came on.

"I don't know about you guys, but that felt weird."

"Yea, it did," Lucky replied.

Erin was standing at the window just past the kitchen area, looking through it; it was still dark on the other side.

"I can't see what's all back there."

"Will the Light Bender open the door?" Emeric asked.

"Lucky," Erin asked, "put the module in front of it. What does it say?"

Lucky pointed the module at the electronic entry lock.

"It says Security Clearance Code 5. Under that, it says, Key Required."

"I have no ideas," Erin sighed.

"Look." Lucky pointed to the entry lock. "It has something different on it."

Erin and Emeric leaned over to have a closer look.

"It's a round pad with a straight line or slot through it," Erin said.

Emeric pointed his flashlight beam into the elongated slot.

"It's a bit jagged inside; you suppose it's a special key you have to put in, type your code, then put your finger on the touchpad?" analyzed Emeric.

"Well, that would make sense," replied Erin." Every entry system became more complicated. The first only required a fingerprint. The second, a fingerprint and a number code, and now this one."

"We've been down here for a long time. Why don't we call it a day? I don't know about you guys, but I'm getting hungry. Maybe we can figure it out tomorrow," Emeric said.

Both Lucky and Erin agreed. Erin took the control module from Lucky and put it in her sling pack with her scanner.

"Let's just leave everything on. Most likely, all the lights will turn off on their own."

They headed down the hall toward the exits. When they got to the first room they explored, Lucky walked in, and the lights turned on. He went over to the open closet, "I might as well take them now." He grabbed the two shirts but left the ties behind.

They all went through the door leading to the staircase, leaving it open. Lucky was the only one who hesitated going up but followed reluctantly.

When they reached the top, Emeric asked, "Do we leave it or close it?"

"We close it. Don't want anybody to discover this when we're not watching."

Lucky removed the wooden bench leg they used to wedge the bookcase door open and tossed it away.

"Since we have power. We should test the red open/close button. I'll stay inside and try it," Erin said.

"No, you won't," replied Emeric. "You have more knowledge of the Light Bender and the module than we do. I'll do it."

Erin stepped out of the staircase entrance, and Emeric took her place.

Erin took the module out of the pack. "I'm ready," she said.

Emeric nodded, then punched the button. The bookcase door slowly moved back into place and sealed shut.

Ten minutes went by. Looking over at Erin, "why has it not opened?" Lucky asked.

"I don't know," Erin stated.

"Maybe you should open it with the module. Maybe the button doesn't work!"

When Erin reached to touch the deactivate button, the module suddenly powered down.

Erin looked over at Lucky with a worried look on her face.

"What, what just happened."

"I lost power...I can't open the door!"

CHAPTER 9

The night went by without incident. Lucky had just finished with the horses and walked into the kitchen. Emeric had coffee, bacon, and Jacks ready to go and handed a plate to Lucky. He sat down across from Erin. "You know, I was thinking."

Both Erin and Emeric stopped what they were doing and looked at Lucky.

"If you don't mind. I want to check out the shower units below; to see if they still work?"

"That's a good idea," Erin said. "Since it's the only shower and restroom down there. Why don't you two use it first?"

"Lord knows you could use it. Just don't get locked in as Em did," Erin whispered to Lucky as she took a sip of her coffee.

"I heard that," Emeric said as he continued to flip the jacks on the grill.

Lucky and Erin exchanged smiles. Lucky shook his head, looked down, began eating his breakfast, and giggled.

"Come on; it wasn't my fault," Emeric exclaimed.

"You broke it!" Erin replied.

"You know darn well that when plastic gets old, it can easily break."

"You still didn't need to punch it."

"I didn't."

"You said you did - when we found you sniveling in the corner on the staircase platform," Lucky said, not looking up from his food.

"Look! It took you three hours to get me out. It was cold on that cement staircase. I wasn't sniveling. I was shivering!"

"I'm sorry," Erin wasn't really. "I couldn't help it. The module lost power. We used it a lot, and the solar panels don't put out much wattage for recharging. I'm sorry you had to wait so long." She tried to hide her smile.

Erin composed herself, "You think you can fix it?"

"I'm pretty sure I can. There's got to be some tools and replacement parts stashed down there somewhere. I'll work on it when and if we find something."

"Okay. If you guys don't mind, I thought we should take turns scavenging the lower level over the next few days. Then take turns at keeping watch here, up top. What do you think?" Erin asked.

"Why can't we all go?" Lucky asked.

Erin looked over at Emeric, "What, ya think?"

"Fine with me. But we should secure the area before we do."

Erin looked at Lucky, pointed her finger, and sternly said, "Do a thorough job."

Emeric interrupted, "what about the section of the lab we can't get into? We still need a key."

Not looking up from his breakfast, Lucky spoke with a mouth full of food. "Erin has a key."

It was just an off-the-cuff comment that stopped Emeric and Erin in their tracks. They turned and looked at each other.

"That's right! I found it in the ammo box."

"What was in the ammo box?" Lucky asked with his mouth still full of food, not paying attention to the conversation.

Without a word, they stared at Lucky. He looked up from his food, lifted his shoulders, and said, "What?"

"The key. The key was in the ammo box!" Erin said.

Lucky shoved a large piece of flapjack into his mouth; pointed at Erin with his fork while looking at Emeric. "You think the key is the one we need?"

"It might be worth a try," Emeric said, looking over at Erin.

"Alright, I'll get it and the equipment." Lucky, when you're done eating, do your recon around town before we head down?"

"Sure, no problem. Are you sure it'll be, okay?" He asked.

"If everything is quiet in town, and we can close the bookcase door, we shouldn't be discovered."

"Okay, then, I'll meet you guys in the tower when I get back." Lucky finished his breakfast and was out the door in a couple of minutes.

When Lucky walked into the watchtower, Emeric and Erin were ready to go. "It's as quiet as a ghost town," he said to them.

Erin touched the Deactivate button, and the bookcase door slid open. Erin was in first, and the stairwell lights came on.

Emeric was the last in, "Don't even," making his remarks to Lucky and Erin, who were both looking at the broken red button.

Erin touched initiate, and the bookcase closed.

By the time Emeric made it to the bottom of the five flights of stairs, Erin had opened the door to the hallway. They made their way to the door at the end of the hall. Erin handed the module to Lucky then pulled the key out of her back pocket.

"Okay, let's see if we get lucky." Both Lucky and Emeric moaned at her pun.

Holding the skeleton key by its large head, she stood looking at the control panel. "This won't work." Erin held up the key, looking at it. She turned it around and around, thinking of other options to bypass the system.

"How about the other end?" Lucky questioned.

"What other end?"

"When you flipped it, the jagged end of the handle is straight and flat. I thought it was just the design of an old skeleton key, but how you held it looked different."

Erin handed the key to Lucky. "Show me what you mean."

Lucky handed Erin her module screen, took the key, and held it in his hand backward. Wrapping his hand around the stem of the key and his fingers on the key head, he put the flat end of the key head into the slot. As he did, the control panel lit up.

"I was hoping the key unlocked a big safe," Emeric remarked.

Erin heard a beep on her module and looked at the screen. The Enter Keycode was gone, and the Deactivate button was now active. She touched the button.

"Lucky, you may have just discovered your first find," Erin said as the door slid open.

Lucky was the first to walk in. And when the lights turned on, they all stood in shock and wonder. They stood in an open hallway; to their left was a set of double swinging doors. The sign above them read *Elevator/Holding*. To their right was a room that looked like an operating room. The sign above said *Hospital Lab*. In front of them, a large window looked into an office area with desks and chairs.

"Where should we begin?" Erin said.

"I think the elevator is the best place to start, possibly something we could use," Emeric said.

They agreed and went through the doors into the holding area. The first thing they saw, straight ahead of them, was a large freight elevator with no doors. Next to it were three sizeable two-door metal cabinets. The wall to the right had a door with a sign above it that said *level 3 Lab*—the next wall to the right; had a set of double swinging doors. Then, to their immediate right, a couple of hospital gurneys.

Lucky went over and started pushing one of the gurneys around. Emeric stepped into the elevator and looked around.

"Erin, Lucky, take a look at this. The elevator control has three pushbuttons; G1, L2, and L3. Think, maybe these are referring to levels?"

"The sign above the door does say Level 3 Lab," Erin noticed.

"Let's take a ride and find out," lucky jumped in.

When everyone was in the elevator, Emeric pushed the L2. The elevator began whining and then started slowly moving up. It stopped at the second level a few moments later, and the lights came on. All three of them stepped off the elevator into what they might describe as amazement. It was a horse stable—six stalls alongside the wall and a door with a *Tack Room* sign and another that said *Wash Room.*

"I know where I'm bringing the horses tonight," Lucky voiced.

"We'll check it out later. Let's head up to G1." Erin said.

Emeric pushed G1 on the control box; The elevator slowly moved up to the next level. When the elevator stopped, the door on the opposite end slid open, revealing a large room.

Emeric stepped out, "it's a garage." The others followed.

It was an oversized garage. One of the garage doors was a double-sized door; the other was a single. Emeric went over and pushed the single-garage door button and the door lifted.

He walked outside and into the middle of the street.

The city hall building and a house across the street were to the north. He turned back toward the garage.

"Erin," he hollered to her. "The whole structure is under a house."

Erin walked out to the street and stood next to Emeric. Lucky followed.

"Looks like they used the house as cover for all the air vents, plumbing, and electrical," Emeric said.

"And the elevator was probably used to transport people from here to the hospital and perhaps also to bring supplies and equipment down," Erin replied. "Let's head back down and check out the rest."

Erin headed for the next double doors back in the holding area when they got off the elevator.

"It has a finger pad scanner." She remarked.

Erin took the module out of her pack and turned it on. When the screen came on, it was the same buttons; *initiate* and *deactivate*. She touched the deactivate, and the double doors slid open.

They walked down the hallway. On the left were three rooms. Each room had a door and a large window. Above each door, a plaque read *Recovery Rooms 1, 2, and 3*. Further to the right was another double sliding door with another finger pad entry. The window next to the door was long and large enough to see all three recovery rooms from inside. Once inside, they looked around, unable to comprehend what they saw.

"Is this the hospital lab like the sign said?" Lucky asked.

"I believe it is. This type of room is similar to what is called a surgical room. However, it looks different from the pictures I've seen," Erin said.

On their left was a door that read Pharmacy. Down the wall were stainless steel counters and cabinets and a door that said Bio-waste. Along one wall were sinks and a wash area with a set of swinging double doors next to them. Another wall had what they could only imagine as hospital machines.

A door led into a room marked *Security/Office* to their right. They could see through the window that it had desks and a long counter with many computer monitors mounted to the wall.

"Em, you want to check out that office room? Lucky, you take the Pharmacy. Oh, and Lucky. Don't touch anything in there. It could be dangerous."

While Emeric and Lucky checked out the other rooms, Erin began exploring the lab and surgical area. Most fascinating to her was a machine above the surgical table with an adjustable arm. As she walked toward the surgical area, the door to her left read *Bio-Hazard Waste*. The door had a fingerprint pad for entry; she would check it out later. Erin walked back by the wash sinks at the far end of the room and pushed through the double doors that said *Laundry*; the lights came on. To her left was a large stainless-steel counter and some rolling hanging racks. The room contained a large commercial-size washer and dryer. Next to them sat a regular household-size washer and dryer. Erin closed the doors and walked back into the surgical area.

Lucky and Emeric virtually popped their heads out of the rooms simultaneously.

"Erin, you got to see this!" Lucky said.

"Lucky, you got to see this!" Emeric said.

Lucky walked over to the security/office room.

"Look at this!" There were six video monitors; they had all turned on when Emeric walked into the room. Each had a picture of a different location outside.

"It's a surveillance system with a control board."

Emeric sat down in the chair and pushed the joystick forward. The picture on the monitor, listed as *Camera-3 South*, moved toward the ground. "See," pointing to the screens. "Each is marked with a number and location. Monitor three is the South camera. When I pushed the joystick forward, it pointed toward the ground." Emeric moved the joystick back, and the camera pointed at the hills to the South. "This will make our job much easier when we're down here."

"But there's still nothing better than having eyes in the field," Lucky said. Watching as Emeric pushed buttons and moved control knobs, Lucky continued, "but it will be fun to play with."

Emeric found the knob that controlled the zoom for the cameras. Lucky thought, he saw a smile on Emeric's face for a moment. *No, that's not possible.* Lucky shook it off.

"I'll be back; I got to show Erin the room full of medicine."

"Okay," Emeric didn't take his eyes off the control board and screens.

When Lucky walked over to Erin, she was moving a machine hanging from the surgical area ceiling. It was white and had a long, adjustable arm; she could manipulate it into different positions. Erin took hold of the handle on the end of the component and moved it around.

"When you grab the handle, it has a trigger switch on the inside. When you push the switch, it releases a lock allowing you to move it around manually."

Erin let go, and Lucky grabbed the handle and tried to move it.

"Your right. It locks in."

He then pressed the switch and moved the arm around. "That's pretty cool. So, what is this?"

They both stepped back to examine it at a distance.

"If I didn't know any better, I'd say it's for scanning someone lying on the surgical table. Lucky looked over at Erin. She had a big smile on her face.

"What? What is it? Why are you smiling?

"Look at the connector at the end of the arm. I think something is supposed to attach to it."

Lucky walked over and touched the stem protruding from the head at the end of the arm. He rubbed his finger up and down it. "Oh, ya. It looks like that thing you have on the tripod."

"It does. It looks exactly the same!"

"I don't understand why?" Lucky asked.

"It's the same reason we've been able to unlock all the security locks for the doors. If the control module operates things down here, then most likely, the Light Bender will too."

Erin swung her shoulder pack around, unzipped it, and took out the Light Bender. Lucky shouted for Emeric as Erin walked up to the table.

"Emeric, you need to get out here!"

Emeric couldn't remember the last time Lucky used his full name. He rushed out of the security room and over to Lucky - just as Erin reached up and placed the orb onto the stem; it locked in place, just as it did on the tripod.

The colored indicator lights on the machine came on. They turned their heads in the directions of the computers in the surgical area as they turned on. Erin looked up at the Light Bender hanging from the head of the arms. All the lights and scanning devices built into the device were twinkling off and on - as if it had activated every capability of the orb.

Erin backed away and stood beside Emeric and Lucky.

"How is this possible," she said. "I knew that if the control module worked down here, then, most likely, the Light Bender would too. But why? How is it possible that what my father and I found so many years ago, and hundreds of miles away, could be connected to this underground facility?"

Lucky and Emeric looked at Erin, then back at her Light Bender connected to the machine.

"It's kinda weird," Emeric said. "But it actually looks like it belongs here."

"I agree; it does. That's why it's so hard for me to comprehend," Erin replied.

"Can you remove it like on the tripod?"

"Well, as you always say. There's only one way to find out."

Erin walked over, reached up, paused, and took hold of the Light Bender with both hands and the orb unlocked. She pulled it off the stem, and the computers at the control center turned off. Erin put the Light Bender back into her pack.

"What now?" Lucky asked.

Erin thought for a moment. "Well, I don't know how you guys feel about this, but I'd like to figure this all out. How about we move down here?"

"I was hoping you'd say that. We want to study the video security system and maybe use it while we're here. Oh, and Lucky found Medicine in the other room."

"Storage units with containers, bottles, and coolers with glass doors," Lucky added.

"We'll need time to go through all this, but before we do, we need to make it look like no one was living in the courthouse building, just in case someone comes around while we're down here," Erin said.

Lucky spoke up, "I'll gather my things and bring them down. While you two are finishing up, I'll check on the horses. I'll set up the second level with water and move them to the stables for the night. If anyone does come around at night, the horses will be safe. And during the day, we can monitor them on the video cameras while outside."

Everyone headed to the elevator to do their work. Once in the cargo elevator, Lucky gave them a peculiar look and said, "Wait!"

"What," Erin said.

Lucky continued, "You think I like climbing five flights of stairs when we have an elevator?" Lucky ran over and grabbed a gurney rolling it into the elevator.

Everyone brought their gear into the garage, putting most of it on the gurney, then rolled it onto the elevator.

"Nice thinking," Emeric said. "This will be easier than carrying everything down the hallway."

Lucky pushed the gurney while Emeric and Erin held the doors open. Emeric took room eight next to the maintenance shelter. Erin took seven across the hall, and Lucky took the living quarter next to Emeric. Each room had a number and a removable name tag that slid into a holder on the door. When everything was in their chosen places, they headed for the elevator to take care of their assigned jobs.

After Lucky had the horses in the stables for the night, Erin and Emeric asked Lucky to head over to the courthouse and do a 'once-over' to make sure it looked like no one had stayed there. Emeric got busy setting up the kitchen; he was in his element. Erin couldn't believe how excited he was going through the kitchen. Emeric would make them a meal for the first time from a stove; she wondered if it would be challenging for him.

They would spend the next four days scavenging the lower level. Lucky was ecstatic when he found a pair of infrared binoculars. Emeric had the best finds. He found a notebook in one of the two desks in the office; probably forgotten; he gave it to Erin and some unused ID cards. Erin learned how to use the scanner connected to the computer on that desk. She was able to download the highest security clearance levels onto the cards. Scanning the ID card over the touchpad allowed them to open any door in the facility.

"Have you got it all figured out?" Lucky asked as he walked into the office.

Emeric was sitting at the video security control center. "Check this out."

Lucky rolled over a chair from one of the decks in the room and sat down beside Emeric.

"Okay, I haven't got it completely, but look at this. Each camera has infrared capabilities…IR. You can turn the IR off or on. Look here at these buttons. If you push the IR1, the button lights up, and infrared is on camera one. Same for each camera, two through four."

"That's cool; show me?" Lucky asked.

"Well, what I've learned from Erin is that the Light Bender has IR. It can sense body heat. So, I need you to test it for me."

"Test it. How?"

"I need you to go walk through town, and I'll turn them all on and see what happens. So, walk around for about 15 minutes, then head back."

"Okay, I'll head up now."

Emeric gave Lucky five minutes to get outside and start walking around. The cameras had been preset to an automatic mode that would begin sweeping the area. Every camera circled almost 360 degrees. Another camera swept its back area as one camera turned, leaving those areas virtually unexposed.

Within 30 seconds of turning on the IR, an alarm sounded. It startled Emeric. Camera-4 on the west side of town picked up a heat signature. Then another alarm sounded on camera-1 on the north end of Amidon; it also recorded a heat signature; it was a person walking around. When Emeric zoomed in, he could tell it was Lucky. The camera automatically followed him. Emeric looked back at camera-4. It was a deer feeding on the grass next to an old building. Emeric reached over and tapped the *Resume/Ignore* button. The camera lifted and resumed its normal scan.

Emeric looked around the board, "how do I turn the sound off?"

Finding the volume controls, he turned Camera-1 and Camera-4 down, then looked back up at the monitors. The other two cameras were still scanning until Lucky moved out of view of Camera-2. Then the alarm for Camera-3 sounded. Emeric reached over and turned the master volume down this time. It had picked up Lucky when he walked out of view of Camera-1. When Emeric glanced back up at the screen, Lucky was gone, and the camera had begun its perimeter sweeps again.

Emeric sat back on his chair, thinking about what had happened. Hearing the elevator, he watched Lucky through the window, swipe his key card and then walk in.

"How'd that work out?" Lucky asked as he walked over and stood next to Emeric and the control board.

"I learned a few things. Except - the camera was following you, then you just disappeared. It must have been when you walked into the garage."

"Erin's Light Bender can see into buildings and through walls. She just turns up the sensitivity level, like that one!" Lucky pointed down at a knob on the control board."

Emeric leaned over and looked at it. "IR Sensitivity. How about that? What do ya say? Give it a try?"

"I'll head back out."

CHAPTER 10

Erin had spent most of the week reading through the notebook Emeric found in a desk drawer at the security office. Much of the writing was difficult to read. A lot of what she called chicken scratching made up most of the notes throughout the book. It was something her mother would always say about something someone else wrote that didn't make sense to the reader. Erin would often talk to Lucky and Emeric about things she had read. She knew they had no idea, but it was a way for her to think aloud.

Erin opened the door and walked into the security room. Emeric was leaning back in the chair with his hands behind his head. She could see he was in deep thought or asleep. Erin plopped herself down in one of the desk chairs and spun it around as she paged through the notebook.

"What's up?" Emeric asked, still looking at the computer screens.

"Remember that book I found in the file cabinets of the main office of the courthouse when we did our first scans? It was about Nanotechnology."

"Ah, ha," was Emeric's reply, still leaning back in the chair, looking at the screens.

"I have a little understanding of Nanotechnology because of the Light Bender. At one time, people could build machines so small you couldn't see them. They called its size a Nanometer."

"Right, similar to the source that powers this facility. You called it…"

"NEMO systems."

"Yea, right, NEMO systems."

"So, in the book, it said that something called Nanomedicine studied how to target an area in the body that the medicine couldn't reach. Anyway, it said that medicines couldn't reach these areas because of something called the bio-barrier. The book said medicines couldn't penetrate it."

Erin flipped through some pages in the notebook. "Here it is. This first part is in large letters. 'WE HAVE BROKEN THE BIO-

BARRIER.' Then, further down the page, it says, 'They are designing the device for control of biological systems.'"

Emeric turned in his chair. "What are biological systems? And who are 'they' referring to?"

"Well, I don't know who 'they' are yet, but biological systems are many different organs in our body called systems, like our muscles. Together they are a system. Throughout our body are nerves that send signals from our body through the spinal cord to the brain; it's called the nervous system."

"So, if I feel pain, it's because of the nervous system?"

"Yes, that's right."

"So, if they can design the device to control our biological systems, then, in theory, they could control our nerves?" Emeric suggested.

"You are on the right track. Here's another entry I found." She flipped through the pages until she found it.

"I won't read all of it, but listen to this, 'The nanobots have manipulated the nervous system. They have attached themselves to the nerve receptacles that identify pain and were able to control the heart rate'"

"So, then it's possible; it could control pain!" Emeric said.

"Listen to this," Erin flipped to the back page of the notebook.

"This is the last entry. It reads, 'The combination of nervous system manipulation and skeletal repair could make a soldier almost indestructible. The nanobots can be manipulated by the orb and controlled by the handheld control device through bio-mechanical transfer. We were forced to add this feature into our surgical technology by the military, so they could control their soldiers or control the enemy.' This part is in capital letters. 'DO NOT LET THIS DEVICE OR TECHNOLOGY GET INTO THE HANDS OF THE ENEMY!'"

"Wait a minute!" Emeric sat up in his chair, "it said the orb and the control device? Could they be referring to your Light Bender and your handheld control module?"

"That was my first thought when I read it. If you think about it, the Light Bender and module have, so far, been able to operate everything in this facility and the manual I have says it's a top-secret tactical device. I just don't know. I'm going to keep reading. Hopefully, I can make sense of some of it."

"Well, what else have we got to do?' Emeric spun around in his chair and played with knobs on the security control board. Erin continued paging through the notebook.

Suddenly, Lucky came bursting through the door, "We've got trouble!"

As Erin turned around, the alarms on two security cameras sounded.

Emeric reached up and turned the master volume down on the video alarms.

"Two riders coming in from the southeast on Camera-3. More riders on Camera-2. They just came out of the hills; a Long-range sensor picked them up."

"You can do that?" Erin asked while looking over Emeric's shoulder.

"The system has both IR and range sensitivity levels," Emeric replied.

"IR," Erin repeated.

"Yes, infrared," Emeric said with a grin on his face."

Erin punched him in the arm, "I know what it is."

Lucky moved his face closer to the monitor. "Emeric, zoom up on these riders on Camera-2."

Emeric zoomed in as close as the system would allow.

"There's a lot of riders in that group," Lucky said.

"You think Marauders?" Erin asked.

"At the same time, Emeric and Lucky said, "Yes."

"Quick, zoom in on the two riders." Erin requested.

One of the riders was slumped over in the saddle. The other riding beside him kept pushing on him from time to time, trying to keep him in his saddle.

"That's Doc!" Lucky yelled.

"What? How do you know?"

"I've only seen them from a distance. It's the same two riders. The other one must be Carlos!"

A sickening feeling came over Erin; she moved closer to the monitor. It was beginning to get dark outside. Soon, the figures would only be a heat signature to the camera's eye.

"How soon will they get here?" Erin asked Emeric.

"I'd say 30 minutes or more. He's having a hard time keeping him in the saddle."

Erin looked over at lucky with a pleading look in her eye, "Lucky?"

"I'm on it. Have that elevator waiting for us; we'll take them right in, horses and all."

Emeric turned and looked at Lucky. "Best, hurry. They're slowing down, and the Marauders are riding hard and fast."

Lucky and Erin headed for the elevator. A few minutes later, Lucky rode out. Erin stood at the garage entrance, waiting.

Lucky was riding hard. He spotted them in the distance. As he drew near, he could see Doc reach down and put his hand on his holstered gun.

Lucky put one hand into the air and hollered, "I'm here to help; Erin is waiting for us."

They all came to a stop. Lucky turned his horse to the opposite side of Doc and grabbed Carlos' arm sleeve.

"Let's go!" They kicked their horses and made a run for it.

When they got to the edge of town, Lucky could almost feel the outlaws beating down on them. He directed Carlos' horse toward the garage. Erin ran over when they got inside, took the reins to Carlos' horse, and led it into the elevator. Doc and Lucky dismounted and followed. Lucky closed the garage door, and before stepping into the elevator, he looked back to examine the area.

A few days earlier, he'd attached a bag of dirt next to the elevator. He reached in, pulled a large handful of dirt out, and tossed the soil into the air. It scattered the area they had just walked. With the floor already covered with dirt, someone would have to open the garage door, come in and look closely to find any tracks. Lucky stepped into the elevator with the others and closed the door, then Erin pushed the Elevator switch.

"What is this?' Doc said with a curiosity he had never experienced before.

"An elevator to a hidden surgical lab facility underground." Erin Replied.

"Surgical, underground?"

"I'll explain later."

As the elevator came to a stop, Emeric was there to help. Lucky ran over, grabbed one of the medical stretchers in the holding area, and wheeled it over. Emeric grabbed Carlos and helped him off the horse and onto the gurney.

They wheeled the gurney into the medical lab as Erin opened the double doors. His shirt and pant leg was soaked with blood. Doc had wrapped a makeshift bandage around the wound to help contain the bleeding.

Emeric and Lucky lifted Carlos onto the table when they reached the surgical table.

"I'll attend to the horses," Lucky said as he headed for the elevator.

"You got this for now?" Emeric asked Erin. "I need to check on the Marauders."

"Yes, go ahead, I got this."

Doc was already working on Carlos while still taking the time to look around the facility.

"I just can't believe this place!" Doc stated. "How'd you find it?"

"That's a story for another day," Erin said.

Doc and Erin removed Carlos' shirt and rolled him onto his stomach. He was in and out of consciousness and still feeling pain. Carlos moaned as they turned him over. Doc had removed much of the compress he had wrapped around Carlos, then slowly moved the material he packed into the wound. Erin noticed how clean and sterile it looked and how Doc had compressed the wrap around him.

"So, I take it they don't call you Doc because it's a nickname?" Erin deducted.

"No, I was a healer, at least as best as I could be with what we had available, which wasn't much. As the years passed, medicine ran out, and so did time. People's bodies had not adjusted to the extreme conditions of living in the wild. Immune systems were dependent on medicines and vaccines…are there any clean bandages or materials? He looked up at Erin. "I need to put new dressings on the wound."

Erin went over to the cabinets above the surgical room counters and opened a set of doors that had a red cross on them. She grabbed a hand full of gauze, bandages, and wraps and brought them over to Doc.

"Here, these should help. Wait before you put it on; I'll be right back."

Erin ran over to the Pharmacy room. When she got back, she handed Doc a spray can; it said; *Antibacterial Spray, an antiseptic agent, provides pain relief and prevents infection.*

Doc took the can and looked at it. "I hope you have lots more of this stuff."

Erin didn't reply.

Doc sprayed the wound before replacing the gauze. Erin helped Doc lift Carlos into a sitting position and held the gauze in place on the side of his back. Doc began wrapping the bandage around him.

As Erin was holding Carlos, his head rested against her shoulder. Carlos softly whispered, "We've only met once – and already, my shirt is missing – you smell…good."

Erin started to reply but realized he had passed out again – she just grinned as Doc finished the wrap. They carefully laid him back down. Erin got a white sheet and blanket out of the cabinets and put them over Carlos to keep him warm.

Both Doc and Erin stood there, looking at him.

"How'd this happen? Erin finally asked.

"We were in the Hills of Amidon when the Marauders surprised us. We made a run for it into the woods, but Carlos took one in the back before we made it to the trees for cover. It was almost dark and, well, you know, Marauders; they didn't follow us. I suppose they figured they would find us later – and they were probably getting hungry. So, I patched him up the best I could. We could see their campfires on the valley floor south of the hills. I watched from the hills, under cover of the trees, for the rest of the next day while Carlos slept.

They had no interest in us yet. They drank so much of their moonshine most didn't get up until noon. Their heads were probably pounding from the hangover. When it started to get dark, I took the chance and headed for Amidon, hoping they wouldn't see us and follow. But they must have spotted us as we made a run for it. If Lucky hadn't come to help, Carlos might have fallen off his horse; then, they would have caught us."

"Well, let me know if you need anything. I'm going to check on Emeric."

"Sure thing," Doc said.

When Erin was inside the security office, she closed the door. Emeric and Lucky were watching the security monitors.

"Em, what's happening with the other riders?"

"They rode into town about 10 minutes ago. They've separated and are searching the whole town. They're so spread out the camera's miss one now and then, but for the most part, the system's keeping track of them."

"Doc said they were in the hills when the Marauders attacked them by surprise. They escaped, but Carlos got shot before they could reach the trees for cover."

"Earlier, Lucky said when he was riding toward them, it was like they knew where they were going – riding straight for our location," Emeric said.

"That's right, almost as if they knew we were here," Lucky added.

"What do you recommend we do at this point?" Erin asked them both.

"We treat them like anyone else. We don't know them yet, so we can't trust them. We watch and listen," Emeric replied.

"That's right," Lucky added. "I think we'll find out soon enough if they're lying."

"What about the Light Bender? Are you going to use it? Emeric asked.

"I'm not sure. Part of me wants to use it to make sure Carlo's is okay. The other says no, don't let them know about it. I'll just have to figure it out as I go."

Erin turned and walked out of the security office and back to the surgical table. Doc was busy sewing the wound on Carlos' back.

"Found some thread and needle in one of the drawers behind me," Doc said as Erin walked up next to him to watch. "The bullet went through mostly muscle and fat, although he doesn't have much fat. It was a clean pass, not hitting any vital organs. However, he's lost a lot of blood; it'll take a few days for him to get his strength back. Lucky for us, he's a stubborn cuss that doesn't give up."

"You know...I am awake," Carlos mumbled.

Erin got a big smile but stopped smiling when she realized Doc was looking at her. Doc smiled and continued working on Carlos.

"I'm glad he's awake," Doc softly stated. Erin could tell he had a deep respect and concern for Carlos.

Doc sprayed some antibiotics over the stitches and then bandaged the wound with tape.

"Time to turn him over so I can stitch the other side." Erin helped Doc get Carlos turned over.

Doc walked over to the counter near the surgical table with the syringe. He pushed the needle into a small glass vile and siphoned out a clear liquid.

"What is that?" Erin asked.

"It's Lidocaine to numb the area around the wound so I can stitch – he moves so much; my stitching job looks bad."

"Come on, Doc, I'm not that bad," Carlos said from the surgical table.

Both Doc and Erin ignored him.

"Your pharmacy room has a lot of medicines that could be very useful and badly needed by other healers, including this Lidocaine." Doc paused and looked over at the Pharmacy room. "However, there's a lot of things in there. I have no idea what they are."

Doc walked over, injected the serum on both sides of the wound, waited a minute, and then began stitching. Carlos grimaced a little from the needle but didn't feel any pain.

"Thanks for taking us in, Erin," Carlos was sincere. "You didn't have to. It's not the way of the Scavenger to trust or help other Scavengers."

Erin shrugged her shoulders. "It's okay. Wouldn't want anyone caught by Marauders." She wasn't sure if that was the answer Carlos was expecting - if the look on his face was any indication.

****

Stryker struck Lucky in the face. Lucky slowly turned his head back, spit some blood onto the floor, then laughed.

"I know who you are. They call you General Stryker. I thought you were dead!" Lucky spit more blood on the floor.

"Dead! Why would I be dead?"

Lucky chuckled, remembering back. "After your men found their belongs in your saddlebags the next morning... I thought they would have killed you!" Lucky gave Stryker a bloody smile.

Stryker punched him in the gut this time. Lucky dropped to his knees with his hands tied behind his back, coughing from the pain.

"So, you're the ghost we were chasing that day. Got to say you were good. I lost a lot of good men that morning because of you. I knew somehow; that something was up. It was only a matter of time until I found the truth."

Still looking down at the floor, lucky chuckled as he spoke. "You were just as confused then as you are now. You have no idea where I came from or how I got here. I'm still a ghost!"

"We've searched every inch of this town. Either you're the only one here, or we haven't found the others yet. And if you have friends here, they'll show up, or I'll find them. And the two we were chasing, one of them is hurt. They won't get far."

Lucky's head hung low, his chin on his chest. "You got lucky. You might see me now, but when you're not looking – I'll be gone."

Stryker grabbed Lucky by the chin, forcing him to look up, "you're no ghost. Ghosts don't bleed."

Stryker removed his hand from Lucky's chin with a forceful snap. Lucky's head fell back toward the floor. But as Stryker began to leave, he turned one last time and, in his typical act of cruelty, kicked him. Stryker's foot made contact with Lucky's arm knocking him onto the floor.

Lucky rolled onto his chest and spat more blood onto the floor; then began to laugh;

That irritated Stryker. "What? What is it you think is so funny?"

"Oh, you haven't seen anything yet. This town is haunted. When midnight comes, so will the ghosts of Amidon."

CHAPTER 11

"What do you mean you haven't seen him?" Erin asked.

"All he said to me was, he was going out to have a look around. You know how he is – he always wants to know what's going on. I'm sure he's ok - no matter what he's doing."

"All right. Maybe I'm just a little stressed with Doc and Carlos here and the Marauders just outside; I'm sure he's fine. Would you still check the security cameras for any sign of him? I'm going to show Doc and Carlos to some rooms down the hall. I'll check back with you when I get them settled."

Erin helped Doc take Carlos down the hall to a room further down from theirs. She reached over and opened the door to room number three. She tried to move forward into it, but no one else was moving. Both Doc and Carlos' attention were on the room across the hall, room one.

"What is it?" Erin asked.

Carlos looked down at Erin. The room across the hall has Doc's name on it."

What?" Erin questioned as she lifted her head over Carlos's broad shoulders to look at the door. "That's unexpected!"

"Let's get Carlos into the room. He needs rest." Doc insisted.

They moved to the bed and sat Carlos down on it.

"So, Doc," Carlos said while looking up at him. "How is it the name on that door is Dr. R Galloway?"

"I'm not too sure. I'm guessing it must be my grandfather."

"Your father's name was Robert. He was one of the first healers, if I remember?" Carlos asked.

"That's right. My grandfather was a doctor and a scientist. He was the first Robert. I am Robert the third. My father was a young doctor when the destruction came. He's the one that taught me the skills, and as medicine ran out, doctors had to learn other means of practicing medicine. That's when they became known as Healers rather than doctors."

"Still doesn't answer why his name is on the door," Carlos questioned.

"I only remember him as a young boy. Then he went away, and we never saw him again. My father chose not to follow. He stayed to help those he could. He always told me my grandfather had to go away to help humanity survive. At the time, I didn't know what he meant. I never really questioned it – I guess we were too preoccupied with survival at the time."

Doc looked back through the door into the hallway. "This must have been where he came." Doc looked at Erin, "what did they do here?"

"I'm not sure myself. I have a notebook they left behind. They were working with nanotechnology, but to what end – I'm not sure".

"You're familiar with nanotechnology?" Doc asked.

Erin suddenly realized that maybe she shouldn't have said that but then recovered. "I have a book I found on the subject I've been reading."

"It is an interesting subject."

"I'll let you read the notebook I found. Some of it's difficult to understand – but very interesting." She wasn't sure if that was a good idea, but she wanted to know and understand more; maybe Doc could help.

"Carlos needs to get some rest. I'll take my grandfather's room. Tell Lucky thanks for taking care of our horses and bringing our supplies down. Thanks again for the help from both of us."

Erin nodded and waved a hand as she left the room. She needed to check on Emeric and the unwanted visitors roaming around town.

"What did you find?" Erin asked Emeric as she walked into the control room.

"Take a look at this. I'll play it back."

Emeric moved his chair over to the further monitor. Six monitors in all. Four were connected to the highest cameras that patrolled the surrounding area. The other two monitors could be used for other cameras positioned in strategic places or playback. The system recorded everything on a continuous loop. Emeric pushed a button to bring up the playback from camera-4. He reversed the recording back two hours, then pressed play, "Here it is."

Erin and Emeric watched the scene play out. Not realizing how many Marauders were lurking in the dark corners, just waiting and watching. Unknown to him, Lucky moved into a dark corner that was preoccupied. The Marauders' gun stock caught Lucky on the side of the head, and he went down. It was dark, and the camera was picking up mostly infrared images.

"Are you sure that was Lucky?" Erin asked.

Emeric pushed the *pause/play* button and looked up at her. "Well, I guess a Marauder might have knocked out one of his own and drug him off?"

Erin gave Emeric a dirty look, "Okay, fine. What happened next?"

Emeric pushed the play button. A minute later, two other Marauders came over, grabbed Lucky by the arms, dragged him over to a building, picked him up, and carried him inside.

"From here, it gets a little fuzzy. The infrared isn't as clear through the building walls." Emeric put his finger on the screen and narrated what was happening. The narration walked Erin through what happened between Stryker and Lucky without their conversation. "...here, see, they picked him up, walked him into a room, tied his feet together, and left him on the floor."

Emeric stopped the play and rolled his chair back to the control counsel center - pointing to the screens at each of the different camera locations, Emeric laid out his plan. "There are eight that I can count. I would guess that one or two were left at their base camp. If we wait until they are asleep or calmed down, we can take them all out, or most of them, then rescue Lucky."

Erin just looked at Emeric for a few moments before answering. "What do you mean 'take them out?'"

"We've got to do something to get him back. If we don't get him tonight, they will torture him to get the information they want."

"Yea, but...I just can't do it!"

"Can't do what?"

"I've never killed anyone, and I don't think I can. Ever since I met Father Moses, I've had this sinking feeling that I'm not to kill anyone. I understand we should protect ourselves, and we need to save Lucky; I just don't feel right about it."

Emeric looked up at Erin with a grin on his face.

"What? Why are you grinning at me?"

"I understand. I know how you feel. I, too, am tired of all the death and destruction. Maybe even more so, now that I've met Yalonda."

Erin smiled at Emeric.

"Which is why I have another idea and something new to show you. Come with me." Emerick got up and headed for the door; Erin followed.

"I didn't get the chance to tell you both about my newest discovery!"

"What discovery?" Erin questioned as she followed Emeric into the Maintenance/Shelter room.

Erin hadn't taken the time to explore the maintenance and shelter yet. However, Emeric had.

"While getting familiar with the security control system, I decided I should learn how the security system is routed to the backup control board here in the maintenance room."

"And that's why we are here?" Erin said with slight hesitation.

"No, no. Although it is quite impressive, I was glancing around when I was in here, and the other big metal door in the back of the room got my attention."

Emeric walked up to the metal door and stood there for a moment. Erin stood quietly beside him. He grabbed the big round locking wheel and turned it counterclockwise. The lever made a soft bang when it had turned all the way open. Emeric pulled on the door revealing another room with benches, lockers, and another door on the far side of the room with a security lock.

"Well, this is interesting," Erin commented.

"It's a security officer's dressing room," Emeric said. As he stepped in, the light turned on.

"What is it for?"

"It's to get ready to go out on security detail. Here is where they would put on their gear to go outside or to go somewhere – perhaps?"

Emeric walked over to a locker and opened it up. Various tactical gear, a vest, and a helmet were still inside.

"And where does the other door lead?" Erin gestured to the other secured door.

"It's a tunnel. It leads to an old house a few hundred feet away – comes out in the basement. The passage opens to a security door in a closet.

The maintenance room's video system controls a couple of hidden video cameras in and outside the house. Probably used to make sure the area is clear before you go outside.

"So, this is the way we're getting Lucky back?" Erin asked.

"It is, but that's not all."

Emeric walked over to a wall with large metal doors on it. Erin had noticed it but was letting Emeric give her the tour. Emeric swiped his security card in front of the scanner at the side of the doors. The large doors began to open to the inside of the walls.

Erin was in shock or awe of what was before her. Inside a small room was an arsenal of weapons. Guns hanging and stacked against the walls and compartments stocked full of ammo.

"I don't know what to say. This is an enormous find, but...."

"But... I know what you're thinking. So, look at this."

Emeric took down a rifle with a scope and tripod legs on it. "This is what we can use."

"It's a rifle," Erin said.

"Yea, a tranquilizer rifle!"

"A what?" she said in confusion.

"An air or gas-powered rifle that shoots tranquilizer pellets. The small pellets these rifles shoot have just enough sedative to knock out a person for a couple of hours. My father knew about these but had only once come across them. That's how I knew about them. There are only four of these rifles and six tranquilizer handguns. The rest of them are regular handguns and rifles. There are 9's, 45's, and some smaller calibers like .380. The rifles are mostly 7.65, 223, 300 win-mag, and 7.62 chambered for military sniper rifles."

"So why does this rifle look different than the other rifles?"

Emeric handed the gun to Erin. "Because it operates on compressed air or gas. It's quiet.

This one has a compressor on its end to keep it from barely making a sound. This rifle has a 34-inch barrel and can shoot over 1200 yards. It uses compressed air or dry nitrogen, and there are gas and compressed air cases stacked here. This is the best part. It has the *NightWatch50* night scope with self-adjusting laser distancing and positioning."

"And that means what?" Erin asked.

"When you aim the rifle at something, the laser will bounce off that object returning to the scope, reading the distance, wind, velocity, and more. The scope will automatically adjust for those variables – making the shot virtually perfect from any distance or angle."

"Em, the things you know can sometimes be scary."

Emeric took the rifle back with a smile and hung the gun back up on the wall.

"Now, tell me about this tranquilizer ammo we need to use with these special guns you found?"

Emeric got a big smile on his face. Erin looked at him funny. The only time Emeric smiles is when he gets excited about something.

Erin could tell he was eager to test these new weapons out.

"Okay, you're going to like this." Emeric pulled out three different boxes. "There are three different tranquilizer pellets we can use. The pellets are a modern style of a dart with a mini-hypodermic needle. Each has just enough to impair a person's functions – depending on which pellet is used."

"Just enough of what?" Erin asked.

"Serum or solution or something like that. I don't know what it's called. It's all color-coded. The green cartridges in this box are a sedative. It slows down the Central Nervous System causing unconsciousness in 5 to 10 seconds, depending on size and weight. The blue cartridges are comatose. It will put the brain into a coma but requires an anti-comatose serum to wake the subject. I didn't find anything like that here, so we might not want to use this."

"I think that would be wise," Erin replied.

"The last one is red. It is a paralytic relaxant. It relaxes the skeletal muscles causing paralysis. It sounds like it would keep the person awake, but they wouldn't be able to move." Emeric looked at Erin with a devious grin on his face.

"No…we are not going to use that one either – no matter how fun you think it would be."

"Alright," Emeric said in disappointment.

He put the blue and red boxes back and sat the green propellants outside the room. He took two tranquilizer pistols and handed them to Erin. He grabbed the high-caliber nitrogen rifle, sat it down in the security room, then pushed the scanner's button to close the doors to the munitions room.

Emeric took a green cartridge out of the box, "each cartridge has ten propellants. The rifle and the handguns use the same cartridge."

Emeric showed Erin how to load the cartridges and attach the gas cylinders to the guns.

"We'll take an extra cartridge and cylinder with us. We'll have 20 shots each. Hopefully, we'll hit our mark every time. The guns are unproven. We won't know if they'll operate or perform properly. And I don't think we'll get a chance to test them."

"I understand. What's the plan?"

"We'll come out the tunnel into the basement. I'll clear the house first. I'm going to set up on the roof of the building in front of the tunnel house. It has a flat roof with a ledge that will keep me hidden. From there, I can survey the area. It's near supper time. Thirty minutes from now, it'll begin to get dark. Soon they'll start moving out of their hiding places and head back to the house to eat. I'll start with those furthest away – then I'll clear the area around the house. Watch for my signal; go around the back of the bar and watch me from the side; I'll signal when it's clear."

"Then what?" She asked.

'Then, make your way to the side of the house. If anyone comes out the door, take the shot. I'll signal how many might still be in the house if you can see me. Find a way in and take down any that are left inside. I'll watch and keep the outside clear. If you have any trouble, and if you can, lead them outside. Any questions?"

"Got it, give me a minute. I'll be right back."

Emeric waited. Erin never left the Light Bender behind. When she returned, she began opening lockers along the wall. Most of the uniforms and gear used by past security were left behind. She found holsters that held the handguns and handed one to Emeric.

They headed down the tunnel when they had the handguns in the holsters and the rifle slung around Emeric's shoulder. Emeric paused by the door at the end of the tunnel and listened. He couldn't make out any unusual sounds. He handed his rifle to Erin and pulled out the tranquilizer handgun. Emeric unlocked the secret door that opened into a closet in the house's basement. In the closet, he stood listening. No sounds. He slowly opened the door and peeked around it. The room was clear, with no one in sight. He made his way to the staircase and looked up, then made the climb.

Glancing over the staircase coming out of the floor, no one was in the house. As he got to the top of the stairs, he spotted a shadow move across the room from a figure outside the window near the house. Emeric moved to a window to the left of the main door. The window was broken; he slightly peered outside. A Marauder was walking in the grass in the front yard.

The outlaw stopped to look at the tree, enjoying the nice weather with the Sun setting off to the West. Emeric thought it was sweet as he took aim and shot him in the butt. Emeric put his back against the wall as the Marauder jumped, grabbed his butt, and hollered; what the…. just bit me. Emeric counted. One, two, three, four…then heard the man drop to the ground. Emeric turned and looked through the window. Seeing the marauder lying in the grass near the front door, a smile came to his face. "Sweet dreams, sweetheart," Emeric mimicked, then headed for the door.

As Emeric was dragging the man inside the house, Erin came up the stairs. "Look what I bagged on my first time out!"

"You're having too much fun. Alright, big game hunter, let's get to work. The fun's not over yet."

The Sun was beginning to set, and shadows stretched east from the buildings. In 15 minutes, it would be down. Anyone east of Emeric would have a hard time seeing anything against the glare of the sunset.

Emeric made his way to the roof of the building as Erin watched from around the building. About five minutes later, Emeric popped over the roofline. He signaled with his hand to the east and held up three fingers. Then, in the direction of the house, held up three. Erin gave him the thumbs up. That would mean one or two were still inside the house with Lucky.

Emeric watched two of the three men to the northeast, talking out in front of a building about 400 feet off. The third was in front of the courthouse directly east of his position, all easy targets.

Emeric waited. The third man walked toward Emeric's position, turned, and made his way alongside the courthouse. Emeric took careful aim making sure he hit the outlaw somewhere he had thinner clothing, usually the pants. Most of them had been wearing a jacket or vest. Emeric fired. The man yelped - put his hand on the building, started rubbing his leg, then dropped out of view. Emeric couldn't have gotten any luckier.

When he turned his attention back to the first two men, one pointed to the north in a circular motion, and the other shook his head. Going to work your way around the building, are you? Emeric said to himself. Emeric aimed at the man on the right. He would have more time to take out his second target on the west side of the building; it was more exposed. Just as the man on the right turned to go around the building's east side, Emeric fired. The man jumped and was out of view. Since the man jumped, he was sure he was hit and would be down in seconds.

Emeric moved his rifle to the next man. He had stopped and looked at something at the top of the building.

"You guys are making this too easy!" Emeric said out loud, then squeezed the trigger but missed.

The pellet hit the brick building; the sound caused the man to look down toward the sound, then turned around, looking off in Emeric's direction. Suddenly the man grabbed his chest and shouted, Ouch. He was rubbing the sting in his chest when his legs buckled underneath him, dropping him to his knees. Still holding his chest, his shirt bunched up in his fist, his eyes rolled into his head, falling flat onto his face. It would have been more comical if the situation wasn't so serious.

Emeric moved to the other end of the roof. Three down, and all was quiet. No one had seen or heard these men fall. At the house, three men were lingering outside visiting. They must have returned early for supper. One of the three left and walked around the side of the house to the nearest tree. Emeric couldn't resist. He was out of sight from the others. The opportunity to sting the outlaw while he watered the local tree was beyond fun.

"Only wish Erin and Lucky were here to see this one." The tranquilizer pellet propelled from the rifle and found its mark on the rear of the temporary gardener. As the Marauder jumped, his pants dropped to the ground. He tried to pull them up and rub his butt simultaneously. He fell onto his head and flipped over onto his back – arms spread out on the grass and pants still at his ankles.

The other two near the front door heard the commotion and hollered for their partner by name. One Marauder yelled again. When no response came, he made his way around the building. When he saw the other man lying on the ground, he ran over to him. Emeric was laughing so hard the gun was shaking in his hands.

"Why am I the only one who gets to have all the fun?" Emeric said as he took a deep calming breath and pulled the trigger.

The outlaw bending over, checking out his partner, jumped and grabbed his butt. Scratching it, he started for the house. Just then, the third man came around the corner. The drug-induced Marauder took three steps and fell into the other man's arms. At that exact moment, something bit the other on his neck. As he reached up to slap whatever stung him, he dropped his friend onto the ground—dropping to his knees, he passed out, laying over the top of his outlaw partner.

With her back against the outside wall at the rear of the house, Erin checked her handheld module to ensure the Light Bender's setting was on stealth mode. The Light Bender could be used without any lights or sound in this mode. Made from an unknown alloy so dense it could be rolled into a room without a sound.

Erin could use the control module like a remote-control device. She would put the Light Bender on the ground and send it in to a room or open area. It could scan as it rolled, sending back 3-D images of everything around it. When finished, she would touch the retrieve button, and the orb-shaped Light Bender would automatically find its way back to the control module.

Erin stepped onto the staircase leading up to the house's back door. She turned the handle on the door - it was unlocked. She slowly opened the door just enough to place her Light Bender on the floor. Still standing on the stairs, the orb rolled into the room. The room was empty. However, the scanner picked up two heat signatures in the front and side rooms. That heat signature was lying on the floor. No doubt that would be Lucky. She moved the Light Bender over to the open doorway leading into the main room and scanned two figures near the front door. They were both peering outside but stayed within the house.

Erin laid down the control module on the steps, opened the door slightly more, and stepped inside. She stopped to listen. She could hear the two men in the other room. One of them was yelling at the other, telling him to get outside and see what was going on in no specific terms. The other was hesitating by arguing back. Erin looked down at her tranquilizer gun. It was loaded, and the safety was off. She positioned herself on the edge of the door jam.

The shot hit the first marauder square in the back. He jumped, reaching around his back, trying to feel what hit as he turned. Erin had the second mark in her sights and fired. The tranquilizer pellet hit the other man in the arm as he turned in reaction to the first, who was still complaining about something that stung him as he dropped to the floor. At the same time, another pellet from behind hit him in the back. He was out before the count of five and would be for some time afterward.

Confused and dazed from the serum, neither one had seen Erin or realized what had stung them. Erin turned and cracked open the door behind her. Peeking through, she spotted Lucky lying on the floor. Erin pushed the door open before entering to make sure the room was clear. Holstering her gun, she made her way over to Lucky. Laying on his side, his back toward her, she grabbed his arm and turned him over.

"Lucky, how are you doing? We're here to get you."

Lucky was sleeping. He opened his eyes. Looking up at Erin, he said, "what took you so long. I was starting to think I might need to rescue myself."

Erin pulled out a pocket knife and cut the ropes that tied Lucky. Groaning from the pain of his beatings, Lucky slowly stood up.

"Where is everyone? He asked.

"Down for the count," was Erin's reply.

"What does that mean?"

"Come on, I'll tell you later."

As Erin helped Lucky through the door, he spotted Stryker on the floor.

"Are they dead?" Lucky stopped to ask.

"No, just sleeping for a while."

"Good." Lucky released himself from Erin's arms and walked over to Stryker. Looking down at Stryker, he raised his head toward Erin and asked, "did they see you?"

"No," I don't believe they saw anything."

"Good," Lucky said again.

"So, you don't believe in ghosts," as he grabbed Stryker's leg and began dragging him to the back room. "Well, we'll see about that."

Erin grabbed the other leg and helped Lucky. When they got to the place, lucky was tied up; they dropped his legs. Lucky took the rope that had tied him and now tied Stryker with it.

"Let's collect up all their guns," Lucky persisted.

They stood there for a moment, looking down at Stryker. Lucky turned to Erin. "Without them, they'll leave town fast. After this, they'll believe in the ghosts of Amidon."

Just then, Emeric came through the front door. Seeing Lucky, Emeric remarked, "glad to see you're alive."

"We're collecting all their guns," Lucky replied. "They'll leave town without them. It'll be a while before they find more."

"Good idea; I'll head outside and gather them up. Meet you at the tunnel!"

Lucky gathered the guns from inside the house. Erin picked up her Light Bender and control module, put them in her pack, and headed for the tunnel.

CHAPTER 12

He flipped Erin over his shoulder, and she landed on her back. Dust lifted from the wooden floorboards. She moaned from the pain but shook it off. She turned over and lifted herself off the floor. She looked at him with determination, then ran at him, hitting him at full force with her shoulder, slamming him against the wall. He grunted from the impact, then lifted his knee and smashed it into Erin's side. Losing her breath for just a moment, she backed off but came back again, throwing her fist at his face. He blocked it. She spun around to put momentum into a backhand fist, but he caught it with both hands. Twisting her arm, he pulled her around toward the wall. With her arm now pinned behind her back, he shoved her against the wall. Her cheek pressed hard against the brick. He held her so tight, she had trouble speaking. She had given up. She was ready to accept her fate. "Do it, do it now if you must. I'm not afraid," She exhaled.

Her pursuer flipped her around, now pinning her back to the wall. He held her arms and hands above her head; she had nowhere to turn. Tired of struggling, she felt more vulnerable than she had ever felt before, for this was it - that moment in her life she thought would never come… Carlos leaned in and kissed her.

Erin quickly sat up in bed. She was panting and looking around the darkroom. Her nightclothes were wet from sweat; she felt tired and bruised. She turned and put her feet on the floor and her head in her hands. It had taken her a few moments to realize it was just a dream.

It'd been a week since Stryker had left. Daily routines were the norm. Carlos was getting better. He was up and moving about—conversations were of general subjects. Lucky diverted his bruised face away from Doc and Carlos to avoid suspicion of his capture and spent much of his time out surveying the area. He found where Stryker had set up his camp on the south side of the hills. They had pulled out not long after they left Amidon.

"Thank you, Emeric," Carlos said. "Breakfast was as delicious as always."

"Glad you liked it," Emeric replied.

Carlos now gave his attention to Erin sitting across the table from him.

"Erin," Carlos said.

Erin almost choked on her food. She was lost in her dream when Carlos said her name.

"Yes?" is all she could spit out.

"I need some fresh air. I'd like to take a walk around town. Would you join me?"

Erin's face turned red. She was embarrassed. She was sure everyone knew what she was daydreaming about. She glanced over at Doc, who was sitting next to Carlos. Then over at Emeric. Neither one was paying any attention. She knew it wasn't possible and was now more embarrassed that she acted the way she did.

Swallowing her food, Erin responded. "Sure. What time?"

"How about in thirty minutes. It'll take a little while to get myself together."

You and me both, she thought to herself.

She looked up. "Sure. I'll meet you at the elevator."

She watched Doc and Carlos leave the room. Erin looked down at her food, then pushed the plate forward and sat in thought.

"Em?" Erin asked. Without having to say anything, Emeric understood her.

"It's a beautiful day outside. It's quiet. Lucky's out tending to the horses."

"Thanks, Em."

Emeric just smiled. He wasn't looking at Erin, yet she could see the curve on his face. He seemed to do that more these days, especially after meeting Yalonda, smiling, that is.

It was a beautiful day out. The air was cool and smelled good. The leaves had changed color, and a breeze swirled through the trees. Leaves fell around them as they walked a while in silence.

"I'm sorry for not making an effort to spend more time with you," Carlos said. "I mean, time together, that is. When I'm around you, I don't know what to say or how to react. You're difficult for me to read. I wish I knew what you were thinking or how you felt. I feel out of place most of the time. Like a fish out of water, I'm sorry. I'm rambling!"

Erin grabbed Carlos's arm and pulled him off the sidewalk alongside an old, abandoned home. It was a small secluded area with a large oak tree shading them from the Sun. The lapped wood siding was once white, but much of the paint had peeled away.

Erin stopped and leaned her back against the house. Closing her eyes, she thought, what am I doing? Those sensational feelings returned. The same she experienced in her dream when she had lost control and given in. She recalled the feeling of helplessness, defeat, and a sense of vulnerability. Then the unexpected happened. The thing she never expected to hope for but knew she always wanted—the touch of his lips on hers.

"Well, I think we got it all, Lucky. Thanks for helping me get our stuff up and the horses packed. And tell Emeric thanks for the extra supplies. I'm going to miss his cooking." Doc said with a tone of regret.

"I know exactly how you feel. I'll tell him." Lucky responded.

Doc threw the saddle on the horse and dropped the cinch belt around its belly. "Carlos should be here soon. He felt he needed to tell Erin himself that we were leaving."

"I think she'll be disappointed," said Lucky. "We were kind-a getting used to you guys being around. And I don't think she spent as much time with Carlos as she wanted."

"I think Carlos was feeling the same way," Doc replied.

He paused in thought, then continued, "he had this unusual dream the other night that he and Erin were fighting, and in the heat of the battle, she kissed him."

Doc lifted the fender and stirrup and laid it over the top of the saddle.

"What do you think it meant?" Lucky asked.

Doc grabbed the cinch strap around the belly, connected it to the buckle, and then looked up. "You know, my father used to tell me that a dream - is the mind's way of communicating with the soul."

"Now, I'm really confused!"

"Well, Lucky. Some would say that our soul knows our needs and desires before we do.

And dreams are the way those needs and desires are communicated. Some might call it a gut feeling."

Lucky got a big grin on his face. "So, like when I get hungry?"

Doc knew he was just funning with him.

"No. I think a little bit deeper than that."

Lucky thought for a while as Doc continued to saddle his horse, then replied.

"I got it. Our soul is communicating this gut feeling to our brain – it's trying to tell us something! Bingo!"

Doc looked over at Lucky with an odd expression on his face.

"Now, that's an expression I haven't heard in a while. Ever play the game?"

"Play what game?"

Doc chuckled, "Uh, never mind. It's not important."

Doc put the stirrup and fender down.

"There, ready to go. Now, where's Carlos?"

Doc and Lucky both looked around.

As they walked back, Erin was holding Carlos' arm. She felt she needed to be closer to him but couldn't. She held him tight.

"I hope you understand? I've got business back home."

"I understand. We all have things we need to do. So, where is home?"

"I have a family ranch south of the Black Hills in the Wyoming Territory. I haven't been back in a while. I need to check on my family."

Erin released his arm and stepped away from him.

"Family? You have a family?"

The projection of her voice and stubbornness tipped Carlos off immediately. He started laughing.

"No, no! You got it all wrong," holding his arms out and shaking his hands. "Not that kind of family. I have parents and a brother; we all work and operate the ranch; I help when I'm home. They're probably getting worried. I've been gone a while."

Erin lowered her head. "I shouldn't have jumped to conclusions."

"It's alright. You had no way of knowing. We don't know each other very well yet. And I, for one, would like that to change."

Erin got a smile on her face.

"So would I."

Carlos took her hand and started walking.

"My brother has a wife and two kids. You'd like her. I think you two are a lot alike."

"Oh, no. I'm already feeling sorry for your brother!"

They were both laughing as they walked around the building up to Doc and Lucky.

"Well, it looks like you two are getting along."

Doc looked down at the two of them holding hands.

They'd forgotten their fingers were interlocked. Untangling them, Erin rubbed her hands together, feeling a little embarrassed.

Doc climbed onto his horse. "Erin," he said. "Thank you for your hospitality and the journal. I'm pretty sure it's my grandfather's handwriting. I'll check and compare it to some of his other writings I've kept. I'm sure we'll have much to discuss next time we meet."

"I'll be looking forward to it, Doc."

"And Lucky, remember our words."

"Sure thing Doc."

Lucky waved at him as Doc turned his horse and trotted off. Lucky glanced over at Carlos and Erin, then headed for the elevator in the garage, giving them time to say goodbye.

They stood next to his horse, just the two of them. It felt as if they were the last two people in the world. She grabbed him. Put her arms around his neck and held him close.

"You will come back?" she asked, almost pleading.

"You know, I will."

"Be careful and keep an eye open for Stryker. Knowing his kind, he'll be back."

"I will; thanks for being honest with me and telling me about him. We were curious why Lucky had been avoiding us so much."

"I was just worried if I didn't tell you, it might put you both in danger again."

"I feel safer already just knowing you care." Erin got a delighted smile on her face, then kissed him one last time.

Carlos took the hat off the saddle horn and put it on. He put his boot in the stirrup, pulled himself up and onto the saddle, and sat there a minute looking down at Erin - and in the fashion of the old west, like a lone cowboy on the trail; he tipped his hat at Erin.

"Ma'am."

She curtsied and replied, "Kind sir, good day."

Carlos turned his horse in the direction of Doc and rode away. Before he was out of sight, Carlos stopped to look back. Not once, not twice, but three times - contrary to the western norm of the lonesome cowboy riding off into the sunset. Erin put her hand over her mouth and giggled. She turned for the elevator, almost skipping, giddy like the schoolgirl she had never been.

CHAPTER 13

Very few crossed the Great River. The land along both sides of the river were prime hunting grounds plush with vegetation. East of the river, very few ventured. Stryker controlled the only access to the east, across the river. He would send hunting parties to track and hunt, but never near the cities.

Ravagers controlled the destroyed cities and lands to the east and west across the mountains, called The Ravage. Cities that once held millions of people are now gone. The planet was laid to waste for the greed of technology. To control technology meant to control the world. The old who survived also called it the Three-Day War. There were no soldiers, no fighting, no hand-to-hand combat, just three days of bombing.

The first day was described as like a storm. Throughout the day, EMT bombs detonated above the atmosphere. It looked like lightning and sounded like thunder. People were interrupted from their daily routine. Shoppers came out of the stores; workers stopped working; students and teachers walked out of their school buildings; masses crowded onto the streets to watch the sky above the clouds.

Minutes later, things stopped working. Cars died on the roads and freeways, most of them still in the lane they were traveling 50 years earlier. Ships adrift on the oceans, planes fell from the sky, and trains became motionless in their tracks – long ago plundered of their goods and supplies.

Day two came the destruction. Through the night and into the third-day nuclear bombs fell. Military installations first, then the densely populated regions, one after the other, nonstop. No one knows if it ended because the bombs ran out or when all the cities were gone; nothing was left.

Many years later, Elders sat around campfires telling stories of a civilization hardly remembered. Stories of old became tales, then myths, and now legends. When the bombs fell, humanity ended.

Months earlier, Stryker and his men were west of the Great River that divided the territories. They were in the hills to the northwest, on a hunting trip preparing for the winter, when they happened upon a party of Wanderers.

****

Having armed themselves with weapons, something uncommon for a clan of Wanderers, they defended themselves against Stryker's outlaws – but not before many were killed or captured. Wanderers were masters at avoiding danger, and if caught by Marauders or Ravagers, the clan would be killed, and everything they owned plundered.

Stryker took no prisoners and kept none alive unless he felt they were young enough to be programmed into the followers he required or tortured into submission as enslaved people. The armed resistance was able to escape thanks to their knowledge of the wooded area, a well-sheltered camp, and their leader, who stayed behind to hold off the outlaws so his family could escape and survive.

He had held the Marauders off for most of the day. Now wounded and dying, they had him surrounded. Stryker had heard stories and rumors about an old man, a remnant of the past civilization still alive when all others were gone. The toll on a man or a woman to survive was heavy. Many barely lived past the age of 50. Stryker noticed this man could be twice that.

The Marauders took over the Wanderer's camp. Items left behind from their hasty retreat made for a comfortable and modest encampment. What interested Stryker the most and why he left this old man alive was because of a rumor.

A rumor told of an old man, a Nomad or Wanderer, who traveled the northern hills and knew of a treasure, a vast horde of minerals and gold hidden somewhere within them. For three days, the old man drifted in and out of consciousness; for three days, they kept him alive, and for three days, Stryker interrogated him with the same question; where is the treasure?

****

Father Moses unknowingly became the treasure's self-appointed guardian as he and his clan traveled the area, keeping watch. His guardianship was two-fold. He didn't know where the Treasure of Amidon was hiding or what it was. Amidon had once been a thriving trading post along the North and the South routes. Wanderers, Scavengers, and travelers passed through Amidon for supplies and to hear and tell the world's news.

Many years before, Father Moses was known as Eli and became a family member of a clan of Wanderers. They often passed through Amidon, staying for a couple of days at a time, trading and visiting with the residents and other travelers. Even then, the inhabitants were old and sickly. Famine and disease took their toll. Slowly they passed on or moved on. Eli befriended a man older than he. He called himself a scientist and a doctor of medicine. Eli just called him Doc.

From Doc, Eli had learned some essential healing. Not much, but just enough to help them in their travels. He didn't know about the secret laboratory, and when he would ask Doc about the work he did in Amidon, Doc would say he was trying to find a way to save humanity. As the years passed, Eli noticed fewer people in Amidon. He asked Doc, where has everyone gone? Doc replied that most had passed away, and the other scientist's bodies were breaking down too fast to be repaired. Eli had no idea what Doc was referring to; even then, Doc was much older than Eli. Sometime later, he learned that Wanderers and Travelers stopped passing through Amidon; trade routes were exhausted, and the towns to the north were now uninhabited.

One last time Eli decided to visit Amidon. He wanted to find out if his friend Doc would still be there. As Eli walked into town, as always, Doc met him on the street. How Doc knew Eli was in town was a mystery, every time he met him on the road, Doc would say it was just a coincidence.

This time everything was different. Doc and Eli sat in the old bar as they had done for many years. Now the bar was empty; dust had settled onto the furniture.

"Eli, this will be our last visit," Doc said.

"I don't understand. Where has everyone gone, and why are you leaving?" Eli was concerned.

"I'm very old, Eli. My time here is almost done. We've completed as much as we could with the time we had left. You've been a good friend. I have always looked forward to our visits and the news you gathered during your travels. I hope you will be around this area for many years to come and that you will check up on Amidon every once in a while. Maybe think of me and remember the good times we shared here?"

"You can count on me, Doc. We travel this area quite often and probably will continue to do so," Eli replied.

"Good, I have something for you. You have learned much about medicine and healing, field medicine we call it. It has helped you and your clan when someone gets sick or gets hurt, true?"

"Yes, that's true, Doc."

"What I have for you is medicine."

"I will use it wisely," Eli quickly responded.

"No, Eli. This medicine is for you. I want to give it only to you. This medicine will help keep you healthy. It will help keep you from getting sick, so when others get sick, you will not. This way, you can help others even more. Do you understand?"

"I do. What is it? Does it have a name?"

"As I said, it will help keep you healthy, and the name, well, that's not important right now. I am giving you a shot that has the medicine in it."

"I haven't had a shot since I was young.

Doc took the air-powered injector out of his bag and stood up behind Eli, tilted his head a little to the side, and in a brief moment, Eli felt a little prick on the side of his neck.

"Not so bad, was it?" Doc said with a smile as he put the injector away and sat down.

"No, that was easy. Will I need more?"

"No, you won't, Eli. The medicine I gave to you will last you a lifetime."

"Thanks, Doc; you know what? I'm already feeling good."

"Great, the medicines are working."

Doc and Eli visited for a while about current events, places Eli had been, and people he had met, but Doc had one last request of Eli before they parted ways.

"Eli, this will probably be our last time together. My work here as a doctor and scientist has taken a long time. I couldn't have imagined how long it would take. However, it's not complete. Someday a person might come to Amidon that will finish our work. They do not know this now and probably won't know it then either, but they will be chosen.

"Chosen? Chosen by who?" Eli replied.

"Well, chosen by a greater power, I hope."

"And what will this 'chosen one' finish?"

"This person will find a key to a treasure hidden away; a treasure so great it will help humanity survive. With this, they will finish the work we began so many years ago. Eli, you are a wise man. Tell no one of this key or treasure it must remain secret. Knowledge of this will only lead to greed, death, and destruction. In your travels and through this area, watch and listen. More likely than not, this person will cross your path someday. By then, I believe you will have the knowledge and wisdom to help lead this person on their chosen quest."

Eli and Doc stood up from the table, and Doc handed Eli a gold bar.

Eli was speechless, "I don't know what to say?"

"You don't have to say anything. This 2oz gold bar is a gift for you and your people. It is a remnant of the treasure."

"Thank you, Doc!"

Eli shook Doc's hand firmly, "I am now the elder and leader of my clan. They have named me Father Moses. It could be partly from my healing knowledge; they call me Moses. But to you, Doc, I will always be Eli.

"Goodbye, my old friend. I will tell no one of this, and I will watch for you until my dying day. You can trust in me."

With that, Doc and Eli parted ways. Unbeknownst to Eli, some thirty years later, at the age of over 100, he would die not from old age but rather from an enemy's bullet.

****

Stryker set up camp in the hills south of Amidon to search for the treasure and watch for other possible searchers. He was sure these were the hills the old man had referred to. Just being in this area and close to Amidon was unsettling. He couldn't get the old man's words out of his head. Before he died, he grabbed his shirt collar and pulled him in close so that Stryker could hear his whisper.

"Remember," he spoke in a soft raspy voice. "Hear me and remember. Good always overcomes Evil. Your thirst for death and destruction will be your own. I'm leaving you now."

"You're not going anywhere, old man!" Stryker replied.

"I'm leaving now for a place I've longed for all my life…my Creator is calling me…home!"

And with those last words, his tight grasp on Stryker's collar released; Father Moses was gone.

Stryker couldn't forget those words. They shadowed his daily thoughts and into his dreams. Every time those words replayed in his memory, he got angry, cursing the old man for telling him to remember. The fact that Stryker couldn't get any information out of Father Moses only made him more determined to find the treasure, and the only clue he had to go on was Amidon.

When he first arrived in the area, Stryker searched the town for clues to the treasure's whereabouts. It was then he had taken the ammo box Emeric and Erin had left on top of the bar counter. Even if the Marauders had gotten there before the scavengers had, Stryker would not have found the clues. He was a Marauder, not a scavenger.

After the mysterious disappearance of his captive in Amidon and his men spooked by tales of ghosts, Stryker was sure there were others after the same treasure. Including the two unknown riders, they attacked in the woods. He was sure he had wounded one of them. The rider had slumped in his saddle after Stryker had made his shot. They pursued the two riders into

Amidon, only to lose their trail. While in Amidon, however, Stryker's men captured the man who led them on a wild chase through the badlands; he referred to himself as the ghost of Amidon.

Having lost their weapons and horses from Amidon's unfortunate events, Stryker and his men made their way back to their fortified base camp. Stryker's fortification was in the Great River's foothills next to the only bridge standing in the territory. Here, they controlled the crossing. If someone wanted to get to the other side, they would have to travel in the water or over dangerous ice in the winter.

Stryker marauded both sides of the river, but few people were in the eastern territories. Hunting was decent to the east, but the further east they hunted, the closer they got to Ravager hunting grounds.

Stryker stood in one of his high watchtowers overlooking the hills and river of his fortified camp. He gazed at the large bridge that expanded over the water: workers and captive enslaved people crossed with crops and timber for firewood and building material. Stockpiles of supplies were coming in for the winter soon to come.

Hunters on horseback crossed the bridge on a hunting expedition. Bison and Antelope were plentiful on the plains. Deer and other small game inhabited the hills and wooded areas. Every once in a while, they would take a bear. The meat was good, and their fur made warm coats. They would soon have supplies to last them through the worst of the winter.

His mind was on the treasure; *how to find it?* He had always gotten the information he needed from the pain and suffering he inflicted on others. He had to find others who, too, were searching. But he didn't have enough men or time to cover the sizeable northern territory. He had an idea as he looked at the bridge that separated the east's ravaged lands from the west. It was risky. He would have to convince them, but how? *Offer them something they need or desire.* "No, that wouldn't work," talking to himself as he paced around the tower floor.

Then again, he was the master of lies and deception. *What if I could offer them something they most desired? What if I could offer them something they needed more than anything else? What if I offered them Life?*

Two days later, and with supplies for two weeks, Stryker and his gang of outlaws crossed the bridge over the Great River, heading east toward Ravager territory. They spent two days roaming and watching until he found what he was hoping for, Ravager hunters. Having organized an ambush to capture the hunters, Stryker ordered his men not to harm or kill them. He planned to show them mercy. If any were hurt or killed, his plan of deception would fail.

All four hunters fell into his trap. Surrounded and outnumbered, they didn't fight as expected. Instead, they laid down their weapons and excepted defeat and death. Stryker was in awe. He had never heard of a Ravager giving up but rather fighting till their last breath. He hadn't expected it to be this easy.

Ravagers are descendants of survivors infected by radiation after the bombs fell. They inhabited towns and cities to the east but only as far as vegetation could grow. Further to the east, the cities and their surrounding countryside were overpopulated. Here, the majority of the bombs fell. Ravagers wore old tattered clothing found within the destruction they lived. Thin and sickly looking, they cared for no one but themselves. Strong-willed and determined to live, Ravagers killed first and then took what they needed. They could have children, but many would die at birth. Children who survived carried the same infections and diseases caused by the radiation. Now that has changed. No longer can they have children. Devastated by a virus, their youngest generation is the last.

They made camp at the spot of the capture. The Ravagers sat on the ground at gunpoint. Stryker ordered those in charge of food preparation to begin cooking even before the camp was all set up. The cooks prepared a potato and pea soup with greens from their headquarters gardens. The main course would be venison, cooked on a spit over an open fire. Near the campfires, the Ravagers watched as the Marauders prepared the meal.

Stryker's intentions were working; the Ravagers were hungry. A couple of Stryker's men took over soup and large portions of deer meat and laid it in front of the Ravagers. Stryker watched from a distance.

The guards moved away from the Ravagers but continued to watch. They looked at each other with confusion, then took the meat and began to eat. Stryker knew they would be hungry. Ravager hunters didn't eat while on a hunt. They would eat wild berries and drink water from the creeks. They never made camp and seldom rested. Their entire trip was spent hunting, day and night, for three or four days until they had all they could carry. Stryker watched as they cleaned their meal to the bone. He walked over with goblets of water, sat down, and reached out with the water. They took it somewhat reluctantly. As they drank, Stryker asked.

"Who speaks for you?"

There was a pause; they looked at each other; their gaze fell to one.

"Why do you not kill us?" The leader asked.

"I didn't come to kill you."

"Why?"

"You are already dying!" Stryker flatly stated.

The Ravager sat up a little straighter and looked at the others.

Stryker continued. "I have come to ask for your help, and in return, I can give you something you greatly desire."

"What? What do you have that we desire?" the Ravager replied.

"Life!" Stryker was lying.

"We have life," one of the others spoke up.

"Yes. But you can't make life," replied Stryker. "You can't make children. You are the last of your kind."

The four Ravagers didn't say a word, just stared.

"I know of something that can help you make life again."

"Give it to us, and we will help you," the leader spoke firmly.

"No!" said Stryker. "I need your help to get it."

"Why do you need it?"

"I don't," Stryker replied. "I want what will be with it, things that I desire." Stryker's false assumption of the treasure was closer to the truth than he knew.

"What do you want from us?"

"I need to find others who are also looking for what we desire. I'll give you crossing into my territory and to the north. Take what you want, but anyone you find, do not kill; you bring them to me, alive!"

"Why do you need them alive?"

"I need information. But what I need next is for you to take this request to your leaders. How long will it take you to travel home?"

"One day," stated the Ravager.

"Good! I must leave for my camp in four days," he lied again. "If you do not return by noon of the fourth day, we will return to our land, and you can live the last of your life."

Stryker motioned for his guards to leave. The four Ravagers stood up.

"We will tell this to our leaders."

They turned and ran into the darkness. Stryker watched them fade into the night, smiling in victory as he turned and walked into camp.

The Ravagers were desperate to solve their pending doom; it made them blind to the deception. Stryker would kill them, however, before they realized they'd been deceived.

CHAPTER 14

Doc and Carlos had gone. No one could guess when they might see them again, Erin hoped soon. Erin spent her days scavenging through the town. Emeric split his time hunting and gathering. When he wasn't hunting or preparing meals, he monitored Erin through the security system in the laboratory hideout or stayed near her as she scavenged.

Lucky was getting restless. The purpose of them returning to Amidon was to find the treasure or, at best, give it a good try. All along, however, he had felt they were kept from their adventure, the search for the treasure.

Something, however, was bothering him, but he couldn't remember or pinpoint what it was – something to do with the house where he was held captive by Stryker. He decided to recreate his capture, hoping it would jog his memory. Standing in the middle of the main street, lost in his thoughts, he turned and headed toward the other side of town. It was the side of town he'd been avoiding, subconsciously not understanding why.

Lucky didn't believe his capture and subsequent beating caused him distress, but as he walked up to the front door, he realized a feeling of dread and doubt had come over him. He had to physically take hold of his right wrist with his left hand. He pushed his arm while pulling with his left just to be able to reach out and grab hold of the doorknob and turn it. He then pushed the door open and quickly stepped inside. Had he not completed that task in one swift move, he might have turned away.

Now inside, those feelings of despair began to recede. He wished he or Erin had killed Stryker; they certainly had the opportunity. He often struggled with those confused feelings of right and wrong. He'd been in this situation before but not this near to death by a ruthless killer.

He remembered Erin untying him and helping tie up Stryker to make it look like he had disappeared; in doing so, he hoped Stryker and his men might believe he was a ghost.

Remembering this gave Lucky a sense of satisfaction; he was beginning to feel better.

As he walked through the house, those feelings began to return. The one thing that bothered him the most began to return. He walked into the room, where he was tied and left on the floor. Lucky stood there for a few minutes just looking down; slowly turning his head, he looked toward the window.

"That's it!" he said out loud.

He sat down on the floor with his back to the wall. It was the same position he sat in when tied up by Stryker. Here, in this position, he glanced out the window. What he saw were the hills of Amidon. It was the same view he and the others saw every day. But it wasn't the hills; it was something else?

"It was the glass!" He almost yelled.

He quickly got up and walked to the front door of the house. As he held onto the door jamb, he leaned forward and looked down the main street of Amidon. He recalled that the first clue in the letter had something to do with glass. He couldn't remember the poem word for word. He just remembered the word *glass*. And although that's all he could remember, Lucky had the feeling he knew where to look.

Erin had always said he lived for the adventure. Lucky practically skipped down the street as he made his way to the bar where Erin discovered the ammo box containing the key, the gold, and the poem, clues that could lead them to the treasure. The same ammo box Stryker now had in his possession.

After leaving the house, Lucky tracked down Erin and Emeric to ask for the paper found in the ammo box. He told them he had some ideas that had come to him while being held by Stryker, and he wanted to check them out. After consulting with both Emeric and Erin, they agreed he should proceed.

Now inside the bar, Lucky walked into the room that had once been the bar's office, the same room Erin had found the ammo box. It wasn't the ammo box nor the file cabinet the ammo box was found under that Lucky was interested in. It was the window. Lucky took the paper out of his pocket, unfolding it; he quickly skimmed, finding the word *glass*.

From in the hills Of Amidon, you will find

*a treasure From The Past For All Mankind.
Where You Found Me look through the glass
Where the x lines up Begins Your Path.*

Lucky walked to the window and could see the hills in the distance. Looking at the riddle, he read, *"where you found me look through the glass."*

"Okay, I'm looking at everything out of the window." He looked down and read the rest of the line, *"where the X lines up begins your path."*

"X? What X?" he looked through the window. "I don't see any X through the window." He said as if talking to the paper in hand.

He pulled out his pocket knife and fiddled with it in his hands. He didn't pick his teeth with it. He had gotten out of the habit from Erin, nagging him any time he pulled it out. Nor had Stryker taken it from him. Even if he had searched and found it, a small pocket knife would have been no concern. Lucky reread the poem, then read the lines two more times. Suddenly he realized he had read it wrong.

Well, not wrong; I just miss understood it. It wasn't an X outside the window; it had to be an X on the window, …where the X lines up.

Lucky carefully looked at every pane of glass in the window, then he found it. So obscure, no one would have noticed it, a tiny x in the upper right-hand corner of the middle right window pane etched into the glass.

Confused about where the X lines up, Lucky moved his head around; closing one eye at a time, he moved his head up then down, all the while looking at the hills in the distance. Fact is, it didn't line up with anything or did it? The X was a little above his sightline. What if the person who marked the X on the spot was taller than he? Lucky grabbed onto the wood window trim for balance and lifted himself onto his tippy toes. As he did, a tall narrow butte came into view.

"Bingo," he softly said. But to make sure, while still on his tippy toes, he moved his head around like before. The only thing the X lined up with was the top of the tall butte. Lucky got excited. On his own, he had discovered the first clue.

Lucky knew Erin was in a building somewhere in town, and Emeric monitored her from the lab. When he got to the control room, Emeric wasn't there. Lucky looked around the lab through the large windows.

Noticing the Shelter/Maintenance room door open, he hollered, "Emeric, you in here?" before entering.

A voice in the distance returned, "In the security room. The doors open; come on back."

Lucky made his way through the room, the HVAC system and piping to the heavy door leading into a room full of lockers that held clothing and equipment for military or security personnel. Emeric was in the munitions room.

"Hey, Lucky," he said as Lucky walked in. "Find anything on your hunt?"

"I did. I found the X that marks the spot."

Emeric put down the rifle he was cleaning and looked up at Lucky. "An X? What kind of X?"

"An X that marks the spot to begin the treasure hunt!"

Emeric could hear the excitement in Lucky's voice.

"Well, I suppose we should go find Erin, and you can tell us all about it."

Emeric hung the rifle on the wall and picked up a Colt model 1911 .45 cal. handgun he had just cleaned, then holstered it. Even with the town secured, they always kept a weapon with them.

Before exiting the Maintenance/Shelter room, Emeric stopped at the backup camera system. In an emergency, the fallout shelter had an exit tunnel and housed all the maintenance controls; water and sewer, HVAC, security systems, and the Nano Energy power source called NEMO Systems or Nuclear Electromagnetic Molecular Operating Systems. A molecular power source that regenerates itself and never burns out.

"She's still in the same building. I have the alarms set if any other heat signatures come into town. I have both security systems operational, so I can move about freely and still be in hearing distance of the alarms."

"Good, let's head over," Lucky said.

Taking the cargo elevator up to the ground level, they made their way to an old wood building just a block away. The signage painted on the front of the building had faded, but the word, *Antiques*, could still be made out. When Emeric and Lucky walked into the old store, Erin was reading a magazine and rocking in an old rocking chair. "Would you look at this! I've only seen a couple of these around. I can't believe this one isn't destroyed or taken from here."

"What you are reading?" Emeric asked.

"Oh, well, it's an old magazine. I found a stack of them behind the counter."

"Really? I can't believe they hadn't been found and burned yet," he said.

"Interesting article. I was just reading about these large art structures made by a local man and placed along a highway east of the Black Hills for people to see. Did you guys ever see them? Eventually, they were dismantled for their metal. "I'd seen them with my father when we first came out West. I always remember they were fun to look at. They made for amusing conversations with my father as we traveled."

"No, I can't say that I did. Spent most of my younger years west of the hills," replied Emeric.

"So, what brings you two here?"

"Emeric looked over at Lucky, who was already distracted and snooping around.

"Lucky!" Emeric lightly yelled.

Lucky came bouncing over.

"Never guess what I found?"

Emeric and Erin looked at each other.

"An X that marks the spot?" Emeric quickly answered, grinning at the same time.

"That's right!" Lucky pointed at Emeric. Already forgetting, he'd told Emeric. "An X that marks the spot!"

"Ok, you got me. What X? And what spot?" asked Erin.

"The X on the paper, in the Treasure Poem with the window."

"You'll have to explain a little better cause we have no idea what you're talking about," Emeric stated.

"Look." Lucky pulled the paper out of his pocket.

"Ok, now I get it," Erin said while looking at Emeric.

"It's like a riddle in a bad poem," continued Lucky.

He unfolded the paper and read, "*Where you found me look through the glass where the X lines up begins your path.*" I was confused at first. I looked all around outside but then realized the X must be on the glass." Lucky paused with a big grin on his face.

"And, did you find it?" Erin asked.

"I did!" Lucky replied. "I looked through the glass, where the X lines up, is on top of a narrow butte directly south of us. I figure about two miles from here. What ya, think?"

"I don't know. What do you think, Emeric?

"I think we need to go see this X marks the spot for ourselves."

"Alright, good, when? Can we go now?" Lucky spit out.

"Well, I guess we could go now if Emeric can," Erin said.

"I'm good to go," he said.

"Give me a moment to pack up my gear, and we'll head over then."

As Erin packed, she thought, I bet this is what it feels like to have children!

After investigating Lucky's find, they gathered around the table in the bar area. Erin sat back in the chair and crossed her arms.

"Well, how do we want to proceed?"

"I'd like to check it out," Emeric said. "It's getting too late in the day for today; it'll start getting dark in an hour. If we rode over and took a look tomorrow morning, it'd give us the rest of the day to explore and evaluate our next move."

"I agree," Erin said.

"Good with me, too," Lucky replied.

"I'm going to head back and work on dinner," Emeric informed. "Should be ready in an hour."

"I'll just head back to the old antique shop and work for about an hour then. How about you, Lucky?"

"I think I'll just sit here a bit longer and think. Read through the riddle some more. It takes me a while to read some words. I want to understand them better."

"Good idea; I'll see you back at the lab in an hour then."

CHAPTER 15

Carlos was seated on a chair when Stryker walked into the room. Stryker's men and Ravager scouts had orders not to kill anyone. However, they had taken liberties with Carlos during his capture, beating him while on the trail. They tied Carlos' hands behind his back and his ankles to the legs of the chair. His face was battered and bruised from days of punishment; his shirt was torn and bloodstained. Between them was a table. The room was dark and damp; the only light was a small window near the ceiling. It was Stryker's interrogation room; even in the future, some things remain the same.

Stryker walked over and carefully sat a box on the table. He then sat on the edge of the table, one leg dangling. Carlos watched as Stryker sat there just staring at the box in silence. Stryker tried to read him, some reaction or emotion, but Carlos remained silent.

"Do you remember it?" he asked.

"Remember what?" Carlos questioned.

"This!" He gestured to the box on the table.

"What? The ammo box?" nodding his head toward the box. "What does it have to do with me?"

"Thought you might have found it while in Amidon?"

"What makes you think I found it, or if I've even been to someplace called Amidon?"

"Because I've been watching."

Carlos didn't respond.

"Over the last six months, I've been patrolling and secretly watching as others came into the area. It just happened that you and your riding partner spotted our camp because some of my men got slack in their assignments. Two of them won't be doing that again!" Stryker gave Carlos a morbid smile.

"I have no idea what you're talking about; why would you think it was me?"

"Because it was with my scoped rifle, I shot you through the side."

Stryker got off the table and walked over to Carlos. Reaching down, he pulled the torn shirt away from Carlos' side. A large scar from the bullet wound was visible, still healing. Carlos didn't look down. He ignored Stryker and stared at the ammo box sitting on the table. Then for no reason other than to be mean, Stryker put his foot onto the edge of the chair and pushed the chair over with all his force. Carlos fell with a thud, his shoulder taking the fall's impact and his head hitting the floor. He passed out.

Carlos awoke from a splash of water, shook his head, and slowly opened his eyes. He was dizzy, and everything was blurry. One of Stryker's soldiers had forced Carlos awake with a bucket of water then two of them lifted him off the floor and up to the table. One of the two men walked out and shouted, "He's awake!" When Carlos's vision began to return, the man standing in the doorway was Stryker.

Carlos mumbled, "how long have I been out? How long have I been here?"

"I don't know," Stryker replied. "Might be a few hours, could be a few days."

"I'm hungry and thirsty."

Stryker turned and yelled at one of his men, "get some water over here for our friend. A man can't talk when he has a dry mouth!"

A minute later, a young man brought a cup of water and sat it down in front of Carlos. Carlos looked up. "Can't drink with my hands tied, and my arms are numb."

The young man looked over at Stryker. Stryker nodded his head.

"Go ahead, Ruger, but only his hands."

Ruger untied him and left the room. Carlos shook his arms and rubbed his hands together. He had to take hold of the cup with both hands before lifting it to his mouth.

Stryker, still standing in the doorway, reached over and grabbed a chair outside the room. He walked into the room, put the chair in front of the table, and proceeded to sit down. Putting his feet up on the table, he pushed back in the chair and stared at Carlos.

"So, tell me about the ammo box. If you didn't find it, who did?"

Carlos didn't speak, just stared at the box, sipping his water.

"When I was first in the bar, no one had been there for years," Stryker began. "About a week or more later, I watched you and your partner ride into town, stay for a couple of days, then leave. I rode into town the next day. The bar had changed; someone had been there scavenging, and this ammo box was sitting on the top of the bar. My men found an old file cabinet in a back room with a hole dug out under it, just the size of this ammo box. Now, tell me. Did you find the ammo box, or was it someone before you? Who found it, and what was in it?"

Stryker waited, feet on the table and rocking in his chair.

"First off," Carlos replied. "I didn't find the ammo box. It was on the bar when we got there. Whoever scavenged the building had taken with them whatever it was they found, if they found anything at all."

Stryker looked at Carlos for a few moments before he got up and grabbed the ammo box.

"Fine. I'll find the truth one way or another," then left the room.

Carlos hoped and prayed that Stryker believed him. He was worried if tortured, could he hold out and not give Erin up.

****

Stryker sat in a reclining chair in his private residence, keeping warm near the large hearth firepit in the center of the room. The smoke lifted into a metal and aluminum stove pipe that exited through the ceiling; the heat from the large fire permeated the room.

Located in the middle of the fortified camp, it was no more than a rustic hunting cabin. Reminders of his wild game hunts littered the log walls. Stryker himself looked more like a mountain man than a militant leader. Animal furs and hides covered the furniture and floor; deer, elk, antelope bear, and birds of many kinds; even a Mountain Lion he had stuffed two winters back. Stryker had been hunting in the same hills of the lion's territory east of the Big River but further away from Ravager territory to the north.

Stryker's thoughts wandered. He was sure his prisoner had more information. He just had to find the right questions to ask. Most captured and held by Stryker told him what he needed to know or die.

Stryker believed Carlos knew about the treasure's legends; he thought anyone who traveled that part of the country knew about the treasure. Every story told might be different, yet each had portions of the truth. If he could piece together enough information from enough people, it could lead him to it.

He decided he didn't have the time to wait for Ravagers to bring him more people to question. Stryker decided he would again set up a camp near the hills of Amidon. It would be faster and more convenient to bring someone captured to the base rather than travel back to the fortress each time. Stryker would have his men prepare to leave in three days.

****

By the time Emeric had breakfast prepared, Lucky had the horses watered, fed, saddled, and ready to go. Emeric had packed enough supplies for a day. He and Lucky had also visited the munitions room. Lucky had admired the .223 rifle Emeric was cleaning earlier that day, with extra-long magazines, a pistol grip polymer folding stock, and customized for fully automatic three-round bursts. He especially liked that it would fit into the rifle case he kept on his saddle. Emeric brought the 1911 .45 cal. and a high-powered tranquilizer rifle for both him and Erin.

After cleaning up from breakfast, Erin and Lucky went to the ground level to finish some packing. Since they decided to be back by the day's end, they didn't need to take the packhorse. Erin put the Light Bender and module into her backpack and had it on her back. Emeric made a pass through the security center to do a quick long-range scan of the hills to the south of Amidon. It looked safe to head out; the cameras didn't pick up any large infrared signatures.

Lucky and Erin were standing next to their horses outside. When Emeric arrived, Lucky handed him the reins to his horse.

"Looks like we're gonna have a beautiful day. Glad the rain we had yesterday didn't turn to snow. The Sun's shining and no wind blowing," remarked Emeric as he stepped up and onto the saddle.

"Any day is a nice day when the wind doesn't blow in this territory!" Lucky announced."

In agreement, they turned their horses to the south and rode out of town. With the butte insight from the Treasure Poem, as Lucky now called it, they took their time to enjoy the ride. They were about two miles from town.

It took an hour to make it to the foot of the butte, but first, they had to make a stop along the way to test Lucky's rifle. Riding past an old portion of fencing Lucky spotted some old rusted metal parts.

"Emeric," Lucky called. "I think I found a great spot to check out this .223."

Emeric and Erin rained in and walked their horses back over to Lucky.

"If we hang that scraped metal on the fence, we can do some target practice."

"Good for me," Emeric said. "Erin?"

"Fine with me. I'm in no hurry," Erin replied.

Lucky and Emeric got down off their horses and handed the reins to Erin. They dug up a few small pieces of metal with holes rusted through. Lucky went over to his saddlebags and pulled out some rolled twine. He cut off a portion with his pocket knife, ran it through the metal's rusted holes, and tied two pieces to the fence line.

"Look at that," Emeric said. "Perfect metal targets."

Looking to the south, he continued. "Why don't we move out about 15 feet and give it a try?"

Lucky and Emeric were ready to try out the new rifle a few minutes later. Erin had taken their horses and moved them further to the south, not to startle them from the gunfire. Lucky set the gun lever to semi-auto, shooting only one round per trigger pull. Lucky squeezed the trigger, and the first ping on the metal target was heard. Lucky took a few more shots, then switched to full-auto. When he pulled the trigger, the three-round bursts startled him, causing him to miss the target altogether.

"Good thing we decided to try the rifle," Emeric commented. "This time, hold the rifle tight to your shoulder and press your cheek into the stock. The gun doesn't have a lot of kick. All you have to do is think of the first bullet making contact with the metal plate. The other two will just follow."

Lucky did as Emeric said. This time all three hit the metal.

"Now, we'll do a sweep. Point the rifle to the left of the target. At the same time, you fire, sweep the muzzle to the right of the target."

As Lucky swept the rifle, one of the three bullets hit the target.

"Good shooting. That'll give you a possible multi-target hit if needed.

When the group arrived at the butte, they surveyed the area. It was a rocky area with hills, brush, and scatted oak and pine trees. The butte was just on the outside edge of the southwest edge of the central hills. Working their way around the tall butte, Lucky found a way up; he hollered and waved them over.

"Take a look at this," Lucky pointed up the path. "Looks like an old path or game trail weaving up and around the butte."

"It's well-hidden too. Look how the path is behind the rocks, and the brush around it makes it impossible to see unless you were looking for it," Emeric commented.

"Wow, I didn't notice that," Lucky replied.

"Let's tie up the horses in that small grove of trees behind us. Hard to say how long we'll be up there; I'll grab the pack of supplies. Lucky, would you grab the extra ammo? It's in the left side saddlebag. I'd rather error on the side of safety than not," Emeric stated.

When they had all the supplies, Lucky led the way up the butte, the path looked more like an old game trail, but they could tell some of the stepping stones were moved into place, making for an easier climb. They took their time not to get winded. As they neared the top, the final 20 feet or more was a sheer cliff. The staircase was carved directly into the side of the cliff, only large enough for one person at a time to climb, a very defensive strategy.

When they reached the top, they had to pass through an entrance that was so narrow Emeric had to suck in his gut and lift the rifle he carried above his head. Emeric ran his hand along a flat seat built into the stone wall as he passed through. Suddenly realizing what it was for, he turned, sat down, and pointed his rifle down the narrow rock ledge staircase. Great guard post, he thought to himself. You can see anyone coming up the stairs, but they can't see you. It took them twenty minutes to reach the top, a small Plateau no more than 30 feet across but well-fortified.

What they discovered was a distant watchtower fortress. Around the perimeter were rock walls. The stone seems too uniform to be natural. The space between the rocks was enough to view and shoot through. In the center of the Plateau was a small stone building. No more than a guard shack. When Emeric walked in, he noticed the old metal stove and a small pile of coal in an old broken box. Those on duty could cook on it or use it as a heat source. On the other side was a small table with two chairs and one partially disintegrated cot.

"Only one could sleep at a time," Emeric said as Lucky came through the door, pointing at the cot. "And look, a stove."

"Nice," said Lucky. "But what's this?"

Lucky climbed up a ladder and onto a wood platform. He pushed open a metal exit on the ceiling above the platform. It opened to the roof. When Lucky stood up, he was waist-high above the opening. From there, he could climb onto the top or just view the landscape around him.

"Looks like a viewing platform," Emeric remarked.

"Sure is. You can see for miles, except for a couple of high sections of mountains to the south and southeast. Glad I brought my binoculars."

The rest of the butte consisted of brush, some wildflowers, and a large shade tree whose roots had grown through the stone walls and into the ground.

Erin strolled over to the shade tree. She sat down in one of the seats made from stone; it was comfortable and cool in the shade. She felt relaxed and content sitting in silence, listening to the breeze and the rustling of the leaves.

Erin hollered over to the boys, "Let's set up our day camp here. The little bit of shade we get will be nice."

They came out of the guard shack. Emeric organized his supplies while Lucky and Erin gathered some sticks and dried brush nearby.

"I'll start a fire in about an hour or so for some lunch. I might need to use it in that old stove if I can't get the coals started. In the meantime, let's take it easy for a bit and talk about what we need to be looking for," Emeric said.

Everyone sat down and lounged around the shaded area of the tree with their water flask. Lucky pulled out the Treasure Poem and handed it to Erin.

"I spent some time reading it, and I think I stumbled onto something," Lucky said.

"What?" Emeric asked.

Lucky picked up a twig and started breaking it, then stated in a slightly embarrassed tone, "you know I don't read so good. Sometimes I turn my numbers and words around or read sentences backward. It was getting late, and I was tired. When I'd read one of the lines that rhyme, I kept starting in the middle. The funny thing is, it still made sense. Then I noticed how many of the lines don't make sense and how the person who wrote it capitalized some words and not others."

Emeric moved over to Erin to look at the Treasure poem with her.

"I just thought it was someone like me who doesn't write very good, but it wasn't. They did it on purpose!"

Erin handed the paper back to Lucky. "Show us what you mean?"

Lucky leaned over, opened his pack, and pulled out a pencil.

"Here, I'll show you." He grabbed his pack, pulled it onto his lap, and flipped it to the backside that was flat and smooth. Lucky started underlining words.

"Some words have a large letter, and some words do not. It looked like it was just random writing, like how I write. Only, it makes sense; mine doesn't. I found that the words with large letters are not as important as the words with small letters. If you put all the words together that have a small first letter, they make a clear sentence."

Erin and Emeric moved over next to Lucky as he drew lines under the words.

"You know, Lucky, I have learned from both you and Emeric that many people who can't read well have more skills and ability than many who can read good," Erin stated.

"Thanks," Emeric said. "That was nice of you to say."

"Ya, thanks," Lucky also replied. "Ok, I'm done. Sometimes you have to reread the words to make the sentence make sense. It's like separating pieces of information, yet there are clues in both. So, you have to use both of these pieces of information to follow the Treasure Poem. I'll read it to you first. Then I'll let you read it and look at it yourself."

"Sounds good," Erin said.

"I read a little slow, but here it goes:

in the hills, you will find a treasure
look through the glass the x lines up on the butte.

place the key into the stone.
view the path it leads to the eagle in the rock.
the key placed within will unlock the entrance door.

Lucky handed the riddle to Erin. Taking it, she looked it over carefully. "I don't think I would have found this. This is unbelievable. Good job, Lucky."

Emeric looked over Erin's shoulder at the riddle.

"Now what?" Emeric asked. "Does it tell you what we need to do here next?"

"Hang on, let me finish," Erin said. She read silently.

If You Are Reading This Letter, You Are Holding
The Key To Life In Your Hands.
From in the hills Of Amidon, you will find
a treasure From The Past For All Mankind.
Where You Found Me look through the glass
Where the x lines up Begins Your Path
From on the butte, This place All Alone,

the key To Life into the stone
view the path it In Time leads to What Is Shone
the eagle And The Directions Are in the rock,
the key Of Life placed within Will Be No More
Below the Eagle slot Found will unlock
Here Too, Find the large entrance Without A door.
A Message, A beware, a warning For The Lesser.
how you use It, You Will Be Measured.
the Key To Life, An Abundant treasure,
will bring – a curse of death or a life of joy and pleasure.

"Here, listen to this. I think this is the section of the treasure poem we need here on the butte." Erin read the sentences as written, then read the underlined parts.

From <u>on the butte,</u> This <u>place</u> All Alone,
<u>the key</u> To Life <u>into the stone</u>

> *view the path it* In Time *leads to* What Is Shone
> *the eagle* And The Directions Are *in the rock…*

"Thanks to Lucky, the way I understand this, we are on the butte already. If we take the key and put it into a stone, it will show us the path to the eagle in the rock."

Erin handed the riddle to Emeric. "So, maybe the eagle is the rock, or…the rock has the shape of an eagle?"

"That makes more sense," Lucky said. "You suppose if we start looking around, we might find where to put the key?

Lucky stood up and started looking around. "Wow, this might take us a while. I didn't realize how many rocks are up here!"

Erin And Emeric stood up and looked around as well.

"It's still early. Emeric, why don't you take care of the meal plans for the day. Lucky and I will begin the search. We'll break for lunch when you call us; then, after lunch, we can all resume the search if we need to."

Emeric went to work prepping the coal stove for lunch and then gathered his supplies to set them up in the guardhouse. Erin and Lucky decided to do their search in a grid pattern. They would push sticks into the ground in the areas they searched.

A little after the noon hour, Emeric called out that lunch was ready. Erin headed to the guardhouse. Lucky wanted to stay behind and finish the grid section they'd begun. He'd just finished his search area and decided to step up onto a small stone on the ground to have a look over the rock walls. Something he did out of routine when securing an area, that one last look around. Lucky turned and stepped down off the rock, then suddenly stopped. "No, they didn't do that to me again?" He said out loud.

He turned and looked at the stone he had just stepped off. What he hadn't noticed was the stone's flat top, making it steady to stand on. He looked up at the rock from which he viewed the surrounding area; it was also a flat surface. This was eerily similar to the window in the bar, where he had to stand on his toes to make out the x on the window pane.

Once again, he stepped up onto the stone, and on the flat surface of the rock, he leaned against it and began brushing the dust and dirt away. His fingers brushed along an indent; it was a hole filled with dust and some debris. Digging out his pocket knife, he cleaned out the hole in the rock. Perhaps the one time, he thought, Erin would approve of him picking at something with his pocket knife. It wasn't a hole; it was a slot in the stone. Large enough to fit a key. He paused with a smile, then headed to the guardhouse for lunch. After all, he was hungry.

Emeric made a light lunch of Bannock bread and venison; he heated it on the top of the stove, along with some wild tomatoes and lettuce still growing in areas around Amidon. Probably leftover gardens of past residents. He called it his VLT; venison, lettuce, and tomato sandwich. He had already begun cooking a stew he planned for the evening meal.

After everyone had eaten and was about ready to go out and resume the search, Lucky asked, "Erin, if you grab the key, I think I found the spot to place the key into the stone."

"You did! Why didn't you say anything?"

"I didn't want to spoil your lunch, and I was hungry,"

"Hang on a minute while I put a few things away. I want to see this," Emeric said.

A minute later, they followed Lucky out of the guardhouse.

"Stand on the stone there and take a look at the top side of the flat stone."

Emeric was the first up. Looking at the area around the wall top, he rubbed his fingers around, touching the slotted hole carved into the stone. He stepped down. Erin stepped up on the rock next and curiously looked at the spot.

"Ok, here we go." She placed the key over the slotted hole and slowly slid it in. It dropped down to where the head of the large key touched the rock. Erin was shorter than the others and had to lift herself onto her toes to look through the key's open head. Lucky giggled.

Both Erin and Emeric looked at him. "That's what I had to do to find the x on the window pane. The people who made these clues didn't take into account a person's size."

Erin smiled and pulled the Treasure Poem out of her pocket.

"Maybe they did, and we just overlooked it." She paused. "Here it is:

...A Message, A beware, a warning For The Lesser.
how you use It, You Will Be Measured.

"It seems this riddle has more to it," Erin continued. "The *Lesser* could mean someone not as tall. So therefore, *how you use it* could refer to the key or something else, like the x, and the phrase, *you will be measured* could also refer to size or height?"

"If it is or if it isn't. Doesn't matter now. We found it," Lucky added.

"OK, you found it; get up and find the rest!" Erin said as she stepped off the stone."

Lucky stepped up onto the stone and looked through the key head to the hills in the distance.

"Wow, I didn't think it would be that easy." Lucky lifted his head, looked off into the distance, and then looked back through the head of the key.

"I can see a rock formation that looks like an eagle's head. But if I'm not looking through the key, I can't see it. The key highlights the shape of the eagle."

Lucky climbed down and let Erin and Emeric take turns looking through the key. Erin opened the riddle, and they all gathered around to read the next section.

view the path it In Time leads to What Is Shone
the eagle And The Directions Are in the rock...

"These two sentences don't make a lot of sense; however, the underline says to *view the path it leads to the eagle in the rock,*" Emeric said.

"Did you see a path? I didn't see one," Erin said.

Lucky climbed back up to look again. "I don't see anything. No path, only the outline of the hills and the eagle."

Lucky put his arms on the top of the rock's flat surface and put his chin on his hands to think. As he looked at the key and the stone, something caught his eye, like a marking. He reached over and brushed it with his hand. It was a marking. He lifted his head, stood up on his toes to lean in further, and blew the dust away from the area with a deep breath. Someone had etched something into the rock, but he couldn't make it out.

"What is it?" Erin asked.

"Something is written in the stone up here. I can't make it out."

"Pour some water on it," Emeric suggested. "Water will make it clearer to see."

Emeric handed Lucky his water flask, and Lucky poured some water over the markings.

"Can you see anything?"

"It looks like markings etched into the rock." Lucky leaned in a little more. "Looks like it says 101E."

"101E? What's that mean?" Erin questioned.

"Hold on; I've got an idea. I'll be right back," Emeric said. "Don't go anywhere!"

Emeric ran over to the guardhouse; a minute later, he returned. He brought with him his compass. Opening it, he pointed it toward the eagle's location. "It's the coordinates of the eagle. It's 101 degrees East. Just like the riddle said, the directions are in the stone. Should have known." Emeric said, somewhat irritated.

Lucky climbed back up and was looking through the head of the key when he startled Erin and Emeric with a sudden burst of excitement. "Wow, what was that? Did you see that?"

"Didn't see anything," Emeric said. "We're down here, not up there."

"You guys watch toward the eagle. Something or someone ran over the hill past the key head as I looked at the eagle. I'm heading to the guardhouse with my binoculars."

"Erin, would you come over and watch the staircase at the entrance to the butte," Emeric asked.

Erin headed over, and Emeric climbed onto the stone to watch. About 10 minutes later, Lucky came running back to Emeric. As he did, they heard gunfire in the distance. "Did you see them?"

"I spotted a few men on horses and some on foot. I counted six riders heading into town. But couldn't make out who they were. I'm guessing Marauders?"

"You won't believe me, but I think we're in trouble. It's Ravagers and Marauders!"

"That can't be possible."

"Well, it is. But that's not the worst of it. A rider was heading our way, but he got pinned down and surrounded. He's in a large rock outcropping straight toward the eagle's head."

More gunfire sounded from a distance. Emeric climbed onto the small stone and again looked over the edge in the direction of the Eagle's Head. "Who would be riding out this way at this time?" he said rhetorically.

"Well, you won't like this, and neither will Erin."

"What?"

"I could see him with my binoculars…It's Doc."

"Doc? What are Doc and Carlos doing back here?"

"It's not Doc and Carlos; I think it's just Doc."

Emeric gave Lucky an undiscerning look, then both looked Erin's way, still guarding the entrance – she looked back at them; she could see by their expression something was wrong - a worried look came over her face.

Emeric lightly whispered, "She's not going to like this!"

CHAPTER 16

They'd give Emeric 30 minutes to get to the ridge about a half-mile to the southwest. It was strategic for him to set up with the high-powered tranquilizer rifles. His shots would be pointing down from the rim, giving him the greatest distance and better velocity. Emeric planned to use the most powerful gun, the single action, to draw the Ravagers out by taking out as many horses as he could from under the outlaws. Horses at that distance were the most prominent targets. It was risky, but they speculated - if Emeric could take out the horses first, the Marauders might stay put, probably use them for cover.

Earlier, they watched Marauders riding toward Amidon. That would possibly leave five or six behind to continue the search. The other concern was the Ravagers. They would be the most dangerous. They didn't ride; they ran fast. Emeric would have to use the automatic rifle next to take out as many as fast as possible.

Once they started to go down, Erin hoped they would focus their efforts on their wounded. Lucky would swing wide around the back of the ridge and come out the other side, riding hard and fast to draw out any Marauders or Ravagers away from Doc. Erin would ride to the northeast, looping around the tree line and into the outcropping of rocks to rescue Doc. Their rendezvous point was the Eagle.

They all had the coordinates, and all were on their own. It wasn't the best plan. They knew the chances of it working would be slim, but Erin would have it no other way. She would save Doc or die trying. After all, if Doc came back alone, without Carlos, something must be wrong. It was selfish, but she needed Doc alive, even if it meant learning bad news about Carlos.

Once they had the horses and gear packed, they set the plan into motion. The three nodded to each other. No goodbyes needed to be said - they knew the risks.

Emeric headed south to work his way to the top of the ridge. Lucky trailed him for a short time, then veered to the southwest to swing around the ridgeline and the southern part of the hills.

Erin waited. It was a long 30 minutes, then came the sound of gunfire off in the distance. Now was her time, and hopefully, the Marauders in Amidon would stay put; they hadn't equated them into the plan.

Erin headed for the tree line north of the diversion and sounds of gunfire. It was a frighting ride, watching for outlaws that may not have been distracted by Lucky and Emeric and for riders coming from Amidon. She would cut south into the hills two miles out towards the location where Doc was holed up or at least where she anticipated he would be.

Emeric couldn't tell for sure. He estimated he dropped at least four of the Marauder's horses. How many more were there? He could not see. He could only hope Lucky would take care of the rest. In the meantime, six Ravagers were below the ridge, just under the position Emeric had concealed himself. Confused, he had already hit three with the tranquilizers, and they slowly passed out as the others watched. Heading toward the gunfire from Lucky, Emeric observed the other three were giving up the chase, doubling back to find the ones that had fallen behind.

Without a leader, four horseless outlaws ran into the woods when Lucky began scattering lead at them from the top of a large boulder. They had no idea he was there; they were caught unaware. Two outlaws still on horseback charged him.

It was a rocky area making it difficult for them to move quickly. Lucky peppered the rocks around the horse's legs with gunfire. Bits of stone and gravel spewed up around the horses. They panicked and bucked. The riders reined in and turned their horses to the west. Within moments of their escape, the two riders slumped over, slipping off their saddles as their horses continued to run off. Lucky looked up toward the high ridge. He couldn't see him, but he knew who it was who shot them.

"Boy, that's some good shooting," Lucky said as he climbed onto his horse. He headed east to the rendezvous to intercept Erin, hoping she had already found Doc.

Erin came out of the trees, moving her horse around an area of large boulders. She had taken out her sidearm watching around every boulder she passed. She'd gotten off her horse and continued on foot, leading her horse, her firearm ready.

"Doc!" She hollered, "It's Erin. Doc, where are you?"

Yelling for Doc was risky. But she might also keep him from mistaking her for a Marauder by giving Doc fair warning. She continued to holler through the boulder field.

"Doc! Where are you?" she yelled again.

"Erin? Erin? Is that you?" the voice came from somewhere within the rocks.

"Doc, It's me. I'm here."

Moments later, Doc appeared from around the corner of one giant boulder. As he did, Erin was caught by surprise as Doc drew his revolver and fired. It happened all so fast. Within a blink of an eye, Erin froze in place, dropped her gun, and put her hands over her mouth. For a brief moment, she thought Doc had shot her. Like many of the stories of the Old West she had read, it was the fastest draw she had ever seen.

When she finally looked at him, he wasn't looking at her but rather at something behind her. It happened all so fast. Even before she could look, a Marauder dropped to the ground almost beside her.

Doc ran over to the man on the ground, gun in hand, and kicked his weapon away. He kneeled on one knee, put his hand over the man's mouth and nose to feel for breath, then touched his neck for a pulse.

"I'm sorry I didn't have time to warn you." Doc stood up and holstered his gun as he scanned the area. "Are you alright?"

"Ya, I'm fine, I think. Maybe a little shook up…I guess. I had no idea he was there… thank you!"

"It's alright. Anyone of you would have done the same for me. He must have heard you as I did."

"Why did he want to kill me?" Erin asked as she stared at the dead man. "I haven't done anything to him. Why do they have a desire to kill?"

"It's not so much a desire, Erin, as it's a way for them to vent their hate."

"Hate? Why? He doesn't even know me. Why would he hate me so much?"

Erin stood in shock and bewilderment. She had fought off marauding outlaws before, but only at a distance. She had never really been this close to being killed by one.

"I asked my father the same questions when I was a boy. As a healer, he was always helping hurt people, many by marauding outlaws. Unfortunately, we buried more than he could heal. He said, 'son, you need to understand…in our world; you will find good and evil. There has been since the beginning of time, and there will be until our world ends."

He paused for a brief moment to look around, then continued. "We've all been given a choice; you are given a choice. You can choose to be good, or you can choose to be evil. If you choose good, you will spend a lot of time, as we do now, trying to make right the wrongs of evil. But, choosing good will bring a life of joy and happiness…much like those feelings we get when helping someone heal.' So, Erin, as evil grows, the heart is consumed with hate, and evil hates everyone and everything. Evil hates someone or something different from itself. That's why another person's life other than their own means nothing."

"We've had to protect ourselves, and outlaws died. I didn't hate them. But, somehow, I felt it was bad!"

Doc looked around again, "We need to go; more could still be nearby. Where are Lucky and Emeric?" He knelt and started to remove the dead man's gun belt. "Look, it's unfortunate in our time and situation that we have had to kill out of self-preservation. A person will either fight or run to survive. We don't kill because of hate but rather to protect ourselves from those who do!"

Erin didn't reply.

Doc stood up, "Erin, we really do need to go!"

Doc packed everything he collected off the outlaw into his saddlebags as Erin explained the diversion plan and rendezvous.

"Well, let's not keep the boys waiting if I know those two. They're probably having some of Emeric's coffee over a fire by now.

It wasn't long into their ride before Erin's thoughts diverted back to Carlos. She had to know.

"Doc, what are you doing back here? Where's Carlos?"

Doc could sense the fear and concern in her voice.

"I came back for your help…"

Doc was cut off when they spotted Emeric on a ridge looking off to the north with Lucky's binoculars.

"Now that's a little strange."

"What's that?" Doc asked.

"I've never seen Emeric ever use Lucky's binoculars. We'd better pick up the pace to catch up with him."

A half-mile later, Emeric was waiting for them.

"What's going on?" Erin asked as they rode up to Emeric.

"Hello, Doc," Emeric said. "Are you both alright?"

"We are," Doc answered.

"Good, because we need to move fast. The Marauders that rode into Amidon earlier are about two miles behind us. I sent Lucky ahead to scout and search our rendezvous point."

With that, they lit out, making their way to the rendezvous point. It was a flat rocky area, one solid rock; the horses wouldn't leave any prints the Marauders could follow. The stone walls around them obstructed views to the east and south. They were still in the tree line, the stones towered over them. Even as they looked up, they couldn't make out the eagle in the rock.

The group moved out of the trees and into the open, watching for the outlaws and waiting for Lucky.

Minutes went by, then Lucky's voice came from behind them. "Glad ya'll made it."

"Where did you come from?" Emeric said as all three riders turned.

"Been here all the time."

"No way, we've been here probably five to ten minutes, and you were not here," Emeric was not happy.

"Well, ok, maybe not right here, but here, just over there." Lucky pointed to the rock wall."

"Lucky!" Erin exclaimed, "we have Marauders on our tail; we don't have time for games. We need to get out of here and find cover."

"Okay, Sorry, just follow me." Lucky lead them toward the rock wall. Then he was gone.

"Woah, where'd he go? He just vanished," Doc said with surprise.

All three stopped their horses. Just then, Lucky peeked around the corner of a rock.

"It's just back here. Keep riding, you'll see."

They realized it was a concealed opening as they rode into the rock. A space led them through a maze of towering boulders that couldn't be seen unless someone rode right into it. They rode out of the labyrinth five minutes later, stopping at the top of a large and long staircase leading down the mountain, large enough to ride the horses down.

"I've thought it but have never said it; You are lucky!" Erin stated.

"I'll never doubt your scavenging skills again, Lucky," Emeric remarked. "How did you find this?"

"Wasn't too hard once I started to understand the words on the Treasure Poem."

"What's a Treasure Poem?" Doc asked.

"That's a tale for another day, Doc; you'll just have to trust me," Erin replied.

Lucky had already pulled out the paper with the riddle on it.

"Here's how I found it."

He read the lines:

Below the Eagle slot Found will unlock
Here Too, Find the large entrance Without
A door.

"I just read it with more than one meaning. There's also truth in the poem by combining the small and large letters together. We know the parts we underlined in small letters say *will unlock the large entrance door*. But the other in capital letters says *Below Eagle Found*, right? So, we are below the eagle we found. The next line is *here too, find the large entrance without a door*. To me, *here too* means-here below the eagle that we found, we will find an entrance without a door. I just started searching around the rock walls only to walk right into this unseen passage."

"Lucky, that is impressive," Doc said. "And as confused as I am right now, you did a fine job leading us here… Spartacus, lead the way."

Then, as if practiced in unison, all three scavengers looked at Doc and said, "who's Spartacus?"

Lucky led the way down the long staircase. Now and then, they could peek through an opening looking off to the south. Most of the time, they were undercover from the outside. They hadn't realized they were so high up in this area of the hills. The staircase led them around the cliffside of a large butte on some of the hills' most elevated portions. About fifteen minutes later, they reached the bottom.

The Sun was setting, and the party was tired and hungry. The path ended in an area surrounded by large stone boulders. Hidden away along the side of the butte was a large open area with grass and a small stream. As they rode into it, they noticed that it had been used before. Along with open spaces, perhaps leading to the outside, was old wooden fencing. Not much remained—just some old weathered posts. Emeric was in the lead and reined in at a grassy area near the creek.

"This looks like a nice spot. I'll have something for us to eat in less than an hour."

It was all routine. Everyone had their job. Erin and Lucky began setting up camp, and Doc helped as much as possible.

It was quiet sitting around the campfire. The sky was clear, with a slight chill in the air. The campfire felt warm and relaxing, it had been a long day, and everyone was tired.

"I'm sure glad you kept the stew you started making for the evening meal. I completely forgot about it; we came off that fortified butte so fast," Lucky explained.

"Well, whatever this stew is, it's delicious. Thanks for making it, and thank you all for saving me. I wouldn't have lasted long if you hadn't been there," Doc said.

"How did you know it was us? You were riding toward us when we spotted you, not Amidon?" Erin asked.

"I didn't know it was you. I saw smoke from a campfire. The butte was closer. The Marauders were right behind me, and my horse was giving out; I wouldn't have made it to Amidon. It was a risk that the smoke was someone who could help me and not a Marauder camp. I owe you three my life!"

Doc looked over at Erin, who was momentarily looking into the campfire.

"Erin," Doc said.

Erin looked up from the flames.

"I know you're worried about Carlos."

Erin slightly nodded her head. Her eyes were tearing up. She was preparing herself for the bad news and kept herself from asking as long as she could, hoping that it would change. But she knew it wouldn't.

Doc continued. "We were two days out from Amidon. We weren't that far, just walking our horses, keeping them rested, and enjoying the nice weather. We decided to cut through the valley of some hills rather than go around them. Doing so would take us further to the south before cutting to the west, bypassing the Black Hills and heading into Wyoming territory. It wasn't but halfway through when we realized that was a mistake. Along the trail, a band of Marauders came from the opposite direction; we ran right into them around a bend and had no idea they were there and probably likewise." Doc paused for a breath.

"I think both sides were surprised we just hung there a moment. Then, we did what we always do in such a situation. As soon as they attacked, we split up. Carlos was on my left, so he turned left and rode into the hills and trees. I went right. It confused our attackers for a moment; normally, they would have to decide who is doing what and who is chasing who. However, it didn't work this time. They all went after Carlos."

"So, do you know what happened to Carlos?" Emeric asked.

"When I realized they didn't take out after me," Doc explained, "I doubled back and followed their trail. Carlos came out into the next valley to the east and turned north, heading back this way. The usual plan is whatever destination we are closer to is where we meet back up. Since Amidon was closer, we would double back to that location. I followed their tracks, but another group cut him off, from what I could tell. And by the looks of it, they were on foot. I didn't realize at the time it was Ravagers. A scuffle took place, but I found no blood, and I heard no gunfire while following their route. I followed them to the far eastern side of the hills of Amidon to their base camp and watched. It wasn't till morning that I could see Carlos, tied to a tree, but alive."

Erin took a breath of relief. "Thank you, Doc, but now what?"

'That's the reason I came back. To get your help. A small band of four Marauders escorted Carlos from camp that next morning. I followed them. They headed mostly southeast. After two days, I knew where they were going. General Stryker has a fortified camp along the Big River. He controls everything in that area, including the only bridge crossing the river. There must be something going on we don't know about. Why do they have a base camp near here? Why are there Ravagers working with them? And why did they not kill Carlos but rather take him captive? Questions I can't answer. I can, however, think of one reason. But right now, all I know is we need to rescue Carlos!"

They all sat in silence. Lucky pushed some wood around in the fire, and sparks bounced and flickered. "Doc, I think I speak for all of us. We're with you on this. We'll help you."

"I know; thank you all; you all have been such good friends. Especially in a time when most people, even those you know, can't be trusted. But the way I see it. We'd need an army to rescue Carlos."

Erin looked at Emeric and Lucky. "Well, if Lucky can bring us some of his Lucky luck, maybe after tomorrow, we can buy an army, and if not, we'll come up with a plan."

Both Emeric and Lucky agreed.

"Good then, let's get some sleep, and we'll continue in the morning. I'll take the first watch."

Morning came too soon. Everyone felt beat from the day before. Emeric had stoked the fire, heating leftover stew from the night before and fresh Bannock bread for dipping into the stew.

Lucky had taken care of the horses but had also taken the time to do a little exploring.

When he sat down with the others, he was excited to share his discovery.

"I found something when I was checking out the area this morning. About a couple of hundred yards, the trail comes out into a large area just in front of a large granite wall."

"Ok, so where does it go?" asked Erin.

"Well, that's the thing. It doesn't go anywhere. It ends there. There's also what looks to be like an old road. It's overgrown, but it's a road if you know what you're looking at."

"Where does it go?" Doc asked.

"Right into the rock wall!" Lucky replied.

"What?" What do you mean into the rock wall?" Erin asked.

"Yeah, I'm telling you right into the wall. I can't explain it; you got to see it."

"Why don't you get the horses ready. Make sure we have some water and jerk along. Lucky, also check the guns and ammo. We don't know where the Marauders are, and we don't want to be unprepared if taken by surprise. I'll clean up here and be over in a few minutes," Emeric instructed.

Everything was ready to go when Emeric got over to the horses. Minutes later, they rode into the large open area. A large boulder blocked much of the view to the south. The extensive cropping of rock pillars and boulders concealed this area from any outside view.

Emeric and Erin got off their horses. She handed her reins to Emeric, walked along the edge of the old road, and then knelt to study it.

"It is an old road, that's for sure. You can see the graveled edge of the road." Erin stood up and looked at the road leading to the rock wall. It seems like they designed it this way on purpose."

"Well, it certainly looks like it ends at the rock wall. Let's go have a look," Emeric replied.

They walked their horses along the old road right up to the cliff wall. The more they looked at it and examined it, the more they realized something didn't fit.

"I know what it looks like," looking straight up the wall. "But I don't want to be the one to say it!"

"It's too flat and perfect to be a granite wall," Doc said.

"I agree," Lucky remarked. "Because it's not a wall. It's a door! A very, very, large door!"

For the next few hours, they explored the wall door, touched it, pushed on it, and banged on it from end to end. Their conclusion, it was still a massive door. However, the discovery they did make was that two doors slide together, making one large closure. You couldn't see the seam that separated the doors because the builders had hidden it in the shape of jagged rocks.

After a while, they all sat down in a shaded area with their backs against the large door, sharing some jerky and water. Finally, Lucky spoke up.

"I'm getting tired of searching for something when we don't even know what we're searching for!"

"Well, that made a lot of sense," Emeric said somewhat sarcastically. "You should pull out your Treasure Poem and find us a way in."

"Yea, well, maybe Erin should pull out her Light Bender and open the…no way! Why do we keep making the same mistakes?" Lucky pulled out the riddle and held it over for the others to see.

"Look, Erin was able to open all the doors in the secret lab with her scanner and module. Why would this be any different?"

"Good point," Erin replied.

"So, look here. We already figured out this part of the riddle, but we haven't used the underlined parts yet.

…<u>the key</u> Of Life <u>placed within</u> Will Be No More
Below <u>the</u> Eagle <u>slot</u> Found <u>will unlock</u>
Here Too, Find <u>the large entrance</u> Without A <u>door</u>.

"The underlined says: *the key placed within the slot will unlock the large entrance door.* We need to find the slot to place the key. And I think the Light Bender can find it."

"You've been holding out on us," Doc began. "It was questionable the things you did and knew; how you found the secret lab and were able to gain entrance to it? It's evident now why you kept coming back to Amidon. And now, you have a treasure map in the form of a riddle. I suspect that is what Stryker is also after. The Treasure of Amidon."

"You're right, Doc," Erin replied. "It's a long story, but there's just not enough time right now. If you trust me on this, we'll share all our information soon. But right now, I need your trust."

"You have my trust; you always have."

"I know, Doc. Thank you. But this is a little different. I need your trust not to talk about or mention what you are about to see and experience… to anyone. And I mean, for any reason! Agreed?"

"Okay, agreed," Doc replied with a curious look.

Erin stood up, pulled her pack around to the front, and unzipped it. All its sensors and lights flashed as she pulled out her Light Bender.

"In all my journeys, I've never seen…what is it?"

"It's what I call the "Light Bender." My father and I found it many years ago. It's a piece of advanced technology from the old world. I've learned to use it in our scavenging. It's connected, somehow, to the secret lab and the treasure. I'll tell you more later but for now, just watch."

Doc just shook his head. "The notebook you gave me to read, the one my grandfather wrote in, he described such a device, but I never understood until now. And now that I understand, we have much to discuss in the future. So, show me what it can do."

Erin handed the Light Bender to Lucky, then took out the control module and turned it on.

"Lucky, I need you to hold it just above your head so I can scan, but I don't want your brain scanned in front of the wall" She smiled at Lucky. "Start on this end," pointing to the left, "and slowly walk alongside the wall door. We'll see if the scanner can detect the slot we need."

Lucky walked to the far left, where the door began. It was the west end of the wall door. Erin nodded her head, and Lucky started to walk with the Light Bender above his head. When he got to the end of the massive doors, Lucky turned toward Erin.

"Wait, stop right there," She said.

Holding her module in front of her, she followed the screen image to the location where Lucky stopped. Doc was standing directly behind her watching her every move. She asked him for his help pointing to a section of the large rock near Lucky.

"Doc, would you go over and touch that large rock right where I'm pointing?"

Doc walked over, put his fingers on the rock, and then looked at Erin.

"Move your fingers over another two inches to the right," she asked.

Doc did.

"Now, push in."

Doc pushed, and a little three by three-inch section of the door moved in. Doc's only words were, "Oh my!"

From here, he understood what to do. He could feel the little trap door just needed to be pushed over. It revealed the key slot they'd been searching for when he did. Erin quickly put her equipment away; they all walked over to examine the key slot.

Erin turned her head and looked at Emeric with a smile. "You were right, all along." She pulled the key out of her bag and handed it to Emeric. "The key is for a large metal door!"

Emeric observed the key for a moment, turning it over a few times. He then placed the key into the slot and whispered *the key placed within the slot will unlock the large entrance door;* he then turned the key.

There was a loud bang, and they all backed away from the wall. It creaked and moaned, then it shook. Dust and debris from plants and brush had grown around the door and along the top began to fall. The doors started to open. In astonishment, they watched. At about five feet apart, the doors stopped. Looking through the opening, all they could see was darkness.

"I may have opened the door, but I'm not going in first," Emeric clearly stated.

"I'll do it," Doc said. "After what I've learned today…what have I got to lose?"

Doc walked up to the edge of the five-foot entrance. He held his breath and took one giant step inside. He felt as if he were traveling through time.

As soon as Doc stepped inside, he stopped. Lights began to flicker. The others walked up to the entrance and peeked in. The lights started to turn on right down the center, similar to those in the private living quarters hallway of the laboratory in Amidon. The lamps on the ceiling here were ten times higher than those in the lab, lighting a path for them. As they looked down the pathway of the light, they could see something at the end: a table and another wall.

"Well, we've come in this far. Any objection to moving on?" Doc asked.

"You got us here so far," Lucky said with a grin. "Lead the way, Spartacus!"

CHAPTER 17

The room they walked through was the largest structure they had ever seen. On either side were outlines of large equipment and other things they didn't recognize. The lights down the center were just bright enough; their eyes couldn't adjust to seeing beyond the pathway. As they walked closer, they could make out another large door. It was not like the doors they had just come through but a large metal vault door. About five feet in front of the massive vault was a table with a large piece of leather draped over it. They stopped in front of the table. The dark leather had faded and was stiff from decades without oil to keep it soft.

"Looks like we need to remove it to see what's underneath," Erin said.

Emeric and Doc carefully lifted the leather cover and set it on the floor in front of the table, revealing a wonderful surprise.

"It's a treasure!" Lucky said, his excitement echoing through the chamber.

On the table's left and right sides were gold and silver bars, five on each side. They couldn't resist; everyone picked up a bar to study it.

Turning a bar of gold around in his hands and feeling the weight, Emeric said, "it's like the same 2oz gold bars we found at the bar in Amidon."

Between the gold and silver bars stacked on either side of the table was a white plastic board with black lettering. Doc picked it up, turned away from the others, took a deep breath, and blew the years of dust off it.

"What is it, Doc?" Erin asked with some curiosity.

"It's a note imprinted on a plastic board. Probably so the letters wouldn't fade."

Doc turned the board over a few times, looking at it and brushing it off a little more.

"It has a message on both sides."

"Are ya gonna read it, Doc?" Lucky asked.

Doc quickly skimmed over the note for a moment, then, wiping a tear from his eye, he said, "My grandfather wrote this. But I'm sorry, I can't read it."

"Why not?" Erin replied.

"Truthfully, it's not mine to read. The way I see it. Your skills and abilities got us here. I look back at the time Carlos and I have spent with all of you; very few could do what you three have accomplished in such a short period. I like to think that a person is chosen to complete amazing things. I've always felt that my grandfather was one of them. Now, more than ever, I believe we are all here for a reason," Doc paused for a moment. "If this is true, then this note has a reason and is meant to be read, but not by me."

Doc reached over and handed the board to Erin. "So, Erin, it's yours to read."

Erin gracefully took the note from Doc and looked at the others before looking down to read.

"It begins with *'Hello, my name is… Dr. Richard Galloway.'*"

Erin looked up at Doc. He nodded his head in approval.

Erin continued to read:

"Welcome to the White Butte Field Base. I was the lead scientist at this base and a hidden

laboratory in Amidon. This field base was named after the highest point above us, White Butte. You are in an underground fortified base designed by scientists, with the military's help to be the last response center if an outside entity should invade our country.

Unfortunately, the devastation came before the base was fully functional. The few of us who survived did what we could to finish for the survival of humanity. We may never know how much of civilization survived after the fall. However, we could only hope and believe that someone would be chosen to lead humanity into a new world after we were gone. It's unfortunate; it would take the destruction of our world to restore our faith.

If you are reading this message, you must be the chosen one. Throughout history, many were selected for great deeds. Some chose to accept their calling; others turned away. Before you is a sealed vault. The table at which you stand around is a small fraction of the wealth and power within this facility.

The vault's vast treasure was not meant to be a luxury for one. It is instead a gift—a gift for all humanity. How you use it will measure who you are and how you count yourself as a person.

Our world's leaders became wealthy beyond recognition. That wealth turned to greed, bringing an overwhelming desire for more. The world's resources brought the advancement of technology, and those that controlled technology had power, and power controlled the world. The vast wealth of this treasure also brings power.

From the beginning, your life has prepared you for this task. Every turn of events, every person, and the signs along the way have led you here. The world is in need, not only of the belief of a better life but also of a savior, a leader to lead them into a new world and a new life.

The wealth, power, and weapons here in this advanced facility are enough to rebuild and save lives with the help of the ADM or Adam as it has been pronounced, 'Armed Defense Military' or Militia, depending on your need or use. However, the weapons at your disposal are not to be used to conquer. Only those who have fallen to the temptations of greed and lust build armies to defeat. The purpose of ADM is to protect you as you rebuild this country's surviving civilization. All this is for the good of humanity. It is a new world, and you now have the means to restore it.

The resources used to defend our country and our borders were removed and dismantled. Wealth and power were used for personal advancement. Technology had progressed to a point where those in power and authority thought no harm would come to them; we no longer had the means to protect ourselves. In secret, this advanced facility was built to preserve and safeguard humankind's remnants after a total collapse of society. However, it was not operational in time. Only through advanced technology were we able to complete it. Your task is to complete our mission by bringing this base into operation to protect and restore humanity.

Begin by determining Safe Zones. Places you deem safe from sickness, radiation, weather, and enemies. Help restore any new cities and help keep them safe. Build homes, schools, hospitals, and churches. Doing this will restore lives, knowledge, health, and faith. Without faith, humanity dies.

An old friend of many years who may be alive today was a traveler in my time. I believe he was chosen by the Creator to be a watchman – to watch for and lead the chosen one along a selected path. I believe this is why you are here today. His name was Eli. He had the heart and soul of a saint. He helped others as he could, learned about essential healing and medicine, and was a friend to all. I believe he was a true prophet of the Creator. We needed him to stay alive as long as possible, and I helped him do that thanks to our work in Amidon.

Through the vault door of this impenetrable base lies the reason the world was devastated and destroyed. No one knew we had taken it. Our enemies bombed every possible location; their goal was to destroy our technology so they could control the world. No one suspected a little town in a state called North Dakota would hide the most significant technological advancement in the world. My friend Eli had no idea what we did here, yet he believed in my work.

Now I'm asking you to believe. You possess the key to life. It does not matter if you take it or leave it. It will find its way back. If you turn away and leave this facility, the gold, and silver before you are yours to take. But remember, wealth brings a desire for more. You might enjoy the pleasure it will bring, but wealth will last only a while, for greed brings lust for power and the curse of death.

IF YOU CHOOSE TO SAVE HUMANITY
These are your instructions.

The key you possess is nothing more than a coded device. However, it is, and always will be, a symbol. The key to life will open more than just a door. It will also access and open every part of your existence through technology, changing your life.

Next to the vault is a coded slot. Below it is a sealed panel. Place the key's coded end into the slot; it will open the control panel's concealed door.

WARNING

Do not push any letter on the keyboard or type in the wrong code. Doing so will begin a lockdown of the facility. You will have five minutes to exit or be sealed in.

If you are the chosen one, then you already know the code. He was a dear friend of mine and now an old friend of yours. He has had many names through the years. He is a father to all. If you know of whom I speak, you are a member of his family. The code is a simple five-letter name.

Once you have entered the code correctly, press ENTER and the GREEN light on the council will blink for three minutes before it deactivates. Place any finger onto the finger pad and press down firmly within that time. You will feel a small prick in your finger. The light will turn solid green. The key to life will activate within ten seconds, and your DNA will pair with the internal security system.

By the sound of your voice, you will command the technology and gain access to the whole facility. Inside the vault, you will find a vast database that will train you on every facet and operation of this base. Once inside, say hello to Sam. Sam is the Systems Analytic Membrane, S.A.M. Sam controls the entire complex through the sound of your voice.

After the coded key is activated, place it into the keyhole located on the vault door...the key to life will unlock more wealth than you could ever imagine and the most valued treasure in the world. Good luck, and may God be with you.

"It's signed: *Dr. Robert Galloway*," Erin said, then sat the message board on the table. Everyone glanced over at Doc. They understood, now, why he couldn't read the message.

"That was a rather lengthy message," Lucky said.

"It was," Doc stated, "but very informative!"

"It explains a lot about many things we've gone through recently," Erin added.

"And I believe the message is referring to you as the chosen one. How do you want to proceed?"

"Give me a few minutes to think," she said, then slowly walked over to Emeric. "The key?"

Emeric pulled the key out of his pocket and handed it to Erin. They all watched as she paced, tapping the key in the palm of her hand. It was a long minute for them. Their anxiety level was high. Finally, Erin walked over to the vault's right side; she reached up and put the head of the key into the coded slot; a panel on the wall slid open, revealing a numeric keypad and a device to place her finger. As she stood in front of the keypad, Erin glanced over to the others as if she needed or wanted their approval. As much as they did, she knew it was the right thing to do. In response to her glance, they all slightly nodded their heads.

Erin took a deep breath and whispered, "Carlos, I'm coming for you next!"

She looked down at the keyboard and calmly said aloud, "Be with me, Father…."

Then she typed his name _ _ _ _ _.

AMIDON, NORTH DAKOTA

The village of Amidon had its beginnings in 1910. It was named after Judge Amidon of Fargo, ND, presumably by friends who wished to honor him. It was supposed to have a railroad terminal, which never materialized due to the end of WWI. It was part of Billings County in the beginning, and in 1914, upon a vote of the people, it became Slope County. Amidon was the temporary county seat until 1916, when it was permanently voted the county seat.

Amidon is located at an altitude of 2,800 feet, approximately 10 miles north of the Chalky Butte Range. White Butte is the highest point in the Chalky Butte Range at 3,506 feet. To the west is the historic HT Ranch which was owned by A.C. Huidekoper in 1884, and the original ranch building is still standing. It rests on the edge of the Badlands of ND, with the Little Missouri river running through the west and north edge of the county.

At one time, Amidon had two banks, two grocery stores, two newspapers, a blacksmith shop, a lumberyard, a hardware store, a theater, a pool hall, a bowling alley, and a ballroom. Also, a Ford agency with a garage, a restaurant, barbershop, livery stable, and gas station. The loss of the railroad and the drought years of the thirties were hard on Amidon and the surrounding area. Amidon now has about 20 people in town. It is still a stopping place for hunters in the fall, high pointers wishing to climb the highest spot in ND, and tourists. Every fall, the town holds an old-time County Fair with 4-H animal shows, a rodeo, and local fair exhibits. The local quilters like to have a quilt show, and everyone likes to drop in for a piece of homemade pie made by the ladies of the Lebanon Lutheran Church.

The mayor is currently Travis Allard, who owns the bar and campground in town. Council members are Rory Teigen, Cindy Ornesby, and Marie Lorge.

Kris Jacobson, City Auditor

ABOUT THE AUTHOR

Rory and his wife, Rosanne, are now retired. They have two beautiful daughters and one amazing granddaughter. Now retired from Oilfield management and retail management for the U.S Olympic Training Center, Rory offset his last seven years in retirement as an amateur historian and tour guide in the Black Hills of South Dakota.

Rory's entrepreneurial experiences have given him opportunities for creative design in both business and life. He enjoys woodworking and auto restoration hobbies and is an outdoor enthusiast.

As a musician, designer, artist, public speaker, and now a writer and author, his first two books are a children's series, "The Misadventures of Alfy and Elfie – Santa's Twin Elves" Rory's third children's book is called the Barefoot Monster. Barry, the Barefoot Monster, also comes in a plush toy, available on Amazon, Barnes & Noble, and at: **RoryForesman.com.**

Watch for more of Rory's adventures through literature.

Made in the USA
Middletown, DE
02 August 2022